DANGEROUS LOVE

Bram Fletcher, vet and lifeboat man, appears in Emergency Nurse Practitioner Regan Tyler's A&E department following his daring and reckless rescue of a little girl from a cliff during a raging storm. Despite the fact that she'd loved him once, Regan just wants him gone. But no matter what she does, their paths seem destined to cross, and his presence back in her life threatens to wreck everything . . .

Books by Teresa Ashby
in the Linford Romance Library:

TERESA ASHBY

◆

DANGEROUS LOVE

Complete and Unabridged

LINFORD
Leicester

First published in Great Britain in 2013

First Linford Edition
published 2015

A catalogue record for this book is available
from the British Library.

ISBN 978–1–4448–2332–5

Published by
F. A. Thorpe (Publishing)
Anstey, Leicestershire

Set by Words & Graphics Ltd.
Anstey, Leicestershire
Printed and bound in Great Britain by
T. J. International Ltd., Padstow, Cornwall

This book is printed on acid-free paper

1

Bram Fletcher stood at the edge of the cliff, the wind snatching his breath away as he looked down into a black pit of nothingness. Out to sea, the inshore lifeboat *Molly Jane* rode the mountainous waves, the spotlight the lifeboat crew were trying to fix on the cliff virtually useless in these conditions. They couldn't see a thing.

Len would be doing his best out there, but he couldn't bring the boat in any closer without risking the lives of the crew. One thing Bram knew was that he'd rather be up here than out there. At least here he could do something, because unless the casualty was swept into the sea, the lifeboat wasn't going to have much to do — and he hoped that remained the case. Once in that water an adult wouldn't stand a chance, much less a child. The helicopter would have been useful right now, but it had been grounded by the ferocious storm and so it was down to man against the elements.

'Ready, Bram?'

Ready? Ready to go over the edge of the cliff on a rope and hope to God he was going down in the right place? The woman walking her dog only thought she saw a kid go over. She admitted it could have been a ragged old bin bag taken by the wind, but she wasn't certain. It was dark, pitch-dark, and the torch she carried with her wasn't very powerful. The woman was still here and she was pretty sure — not absolutely sure, just pretty sure — that the kid had gone over just about here. If it was a kid. She thought she might have heard a scream, but it was just as likely to have been the wailing wind.

Bram hoped she was wrong. Far better that the woman walked away feeling a bit embarrassed for calling them out on a false alarm than he got down the cliff and found a body — or worse, no body at all. A lump lodged in his throat and he swallowed it down. No children had been reported missing, which was good. He had no idea of the condition of the child — if there was one — but if he or she was conscious, he could imagine their terror. He turned around and took a step backwards, wedging his feet against the cliff, the torch on his helmet lighting the cliff face in front of him as he began his slow, careful descent. The last thing he saw before he was staring at rock was the huddled, shivering form of the dog sitting at the heels of the woman.

He looked up briefly and saw the beams of torches shining down at him. 'Take it easy, Bram!' Malcolm yelled.

Yeah, right, like I'm going to go fast and risk ending up on the rocks below. He was known for being reckless, for taking risks, but he wasn't about to smash himself to pieces for the sake of a few extra seconds. It wouldn't help the kid, and hell, it might hurt just a little — if it didn't kill him straight away. He

3

didn't mind that — a quick painless exit — but he was no fool and no stranger to pain, so he planned to do everything he could to stay alive and in one piece.

Despite the cold seeping in through all the protective gear, he felt a trickle of sweat run down his spine. It wasn't fear. Once Bram would have been terrified doing this, worrying about the effect his death might have on those he loved . . . *Oh, quit being coy, Fletcher. When you mean Regan, why don't you just admit it instead of dancing around the safe zone?* There weren't many days in his life that he didn't think about Regan and on every shout she was there in his mind, but no longer in his life.

Knowing she was sitting at home or waiting at the lifeboat station going through hell had made doing this job hard. So it was a good thing she was no longer part of his life, right? Yes it was. Yet no matter how many times he'd told himself that over the past six years, there was still a part of him that longed to have her sitting at home waiting, ready with her warm arms and her soft lips when he came home. He licked his lips, tasted rain, remembered how it had felt to taste the tears on her trembling mouth and how bad that had made him feel — and yet how good.

How much further? He looked down and could see the white foam on the waves as they crashed over the rocks below, lit up by the beam from his helmet. What if he got to the ledge and it was empty and the cries they thought they'd heard up top turned out to be a gull? The ice in the wind was inside him now, chilling him from the inside out. They didn't have to be out by much for him to be in completely the wrong place. If there was a kid — and it was a big if — he could be anywhere along here.

Then he caught it in the beam: the dip in the rock, the tiny ledge leading into a shallow hollow, and two small feet — one with a shoe, one without. There was something so joyful about seeing those little feet; and yet at the same time, something so bone-achingly sad. The socks were wet; they were ankle socks with little frills around the tops and skinny legs sticking out of them.

'I see her!' he shouted, and his headset crackled in response. 'It's a little girl.'

'What's her condition?'

'Can't tell yet.'

Lucky to have fallen inwards into the hollow and to find a ledge beneath her, that was for sure. But how far did that luck go? Had she hit the rock and lucked out? Was she where the fall had thrown her, or had she got herself into the dip, as far from the edge as she could get? If she had, then she was a pretty resourceful little girl. He reckoned she was about five years old, maybe younger. Finding any resources when you were that age and scared out of your wits was pretty amazing.

'Give me more rope!' he shouted as everything seemed to suddenly slow down and his progress was halted. The rope was played out and he moved down further. His feet found the edge of the ledge and he went down on his knees and found the kid huddled, sitting upright with her back against the rock, blood practically obscuring her face.

'Hey,' he said. 'My name's Bram. I'm going to get you out of here, honey, okay? You're going to be all right and I promise you, going back up is going to hurt a lot less than coming down did.'

She was crying, her tears making trails through the blood. Poor little kid. She must be terrified. And where were her parents while all this was going on? At her age she should be at home tucked up in bed, not sitting halfway down a cliff just feet above the raging water, all on her own and scared out of her damn wits.

'Can you tell me your name?' he asked her gently.

It took her a while to speak. 'Georgie,' she said at last.

'All right, Georgie. I need to just

check out your injuries, then we'll get
you back up the top.'

'Are you a doctor?'

'No,' he laughed. 'I'm a vet.'

Amazing kid — she laughed as well,
and didn't she have a knockout smile?
She thought he was kidding. Everyone
did, but first and foremost he was a vet
and second to that, a lifeboat volunteer
with Advanced Life Support training.

'Can you tell me what hurts,
Georgie?'

'Everything,' she said. 'But my arm,
mostly.'

She was holding it, making a sling for
it with her other arm. If she'd fallen all
that way and just broken her arm and
got a gash on her head, then she really
was lucky. But kids were unreliable
witnesses to their own injuries. He had
to be careful.

'Anything else?'

'I'm scared.'

'Of course you are,' he said as he
wrapped her in a blanket and tucked it
around her. Her chin wobbled. 'But

there's nothing to be scared of, I promise. I'm going to get you out of here. Does it hurt when you breathe?'

'No.'

'How about your head?'

'Sore.'

'Well I'll tell you what I'm going to do, Georgie. I'll get the guys up top to send down a special board which I'll strap you to, then they'll pull you up, but don't worry because I'm going to be right with you. I won't leave you, okay?'

The blood on her face looked pretty alarming. *Her mother should see her right now and get the shock she deserves,* he thought angrily. *She should see how letting a little kid out on a night like this can end up.* But the chances were that by the time they located her, down the pub or in a nightclub or wherever the hell she was, Georgie was going to be all cleaned up and looking pretty again.

He relayed the information to the team on the ground, including the fact that as they suspected, there wasn't room for anyone else down there so he was on his own. Getting back up with her wasn't going to be easy. He'd not only have to deal with being buffeted by the wind, but he'd have to hang on to her as well and make damn sure he kept smiling just in case she could see fear on his face. It wasn't fear for himself, but for her. The truth was, he had no fear. To fear, you had to love, wasn't that right? Fear was for those left behind.

'What were you doing on the cliff on your own anyway, Georgie?'

'Walking,' Georgie said, her dark eyes like black pools in the torchlight.

'Did your mother know you were out?'

'No!' she rapped out the word. 'You mustn't tell her.' She began to sob.

Whoops, maybe the mother was in the dark about all this after all. Right now she might be sitting at home watching TV, thinking her daughter was asleep in bed. 'It's all right, honey,' he said, putting his arm around her and giving her the gentlest squeeze — not enough to hurt but enough, he hoped, to reassure. 'Your mummy will just be glad you're okay. She won't be mad.'

'You don't know my mummy,' she said, and again there was that gorgeous smile that lit up her whole bloodied face.

Well if she's anything like her daughter, Bram thought, *then she's going to be one tough lady!*

The tears came again, swift on the heels of the smile. The poor kid was in bits.

'Steady,' he said as the board came down and he retrieved it. There wasn't a lot of room for manoeuvre on the ledge and the darkness didn't help, but Georgie was too worried about what her mother was going to say not to be completely co-operative as Bram strapped her to the board.

'It's not just me holding on to you,' he said. 'The guys up the top there are holding you as well. You can't fall, okay?

You're not going to worry about that, are you?'

'I'm worried about my arm,' she said earnestly. 'It hurts a lot.'

She seemed a lot older than the estimated five years, but she was a tiny little scrap of a thing. She had an unusual combination of big blue eyes and dark chocolate-brown hair, and without all that blood on her face, Bram guessed she'd be a pretty little lass.

The journey up was easier. The wind wasn't any less vicious and the cold was just as penetrating, but all Bram had to watch for was jagged areas of rock where the ropes might snag or even knock into the board. And when he looked up he could see the shadow of an ice-blue flashing light. The ambulance had arrived and with it the paramedics, who would be able to do far more for this little girl than he could.

He'd cooled down about the mother too, imagining the state she'd be in when she found out. He wouldn't mind betting Georgie was a bit of a handful.

When they reached the top, hands reached out to pull Georgie up onto the land and she was obscured from Bram's view by the jacket of a paramedic. Another hand reached out and gripped Bram's wrist, helping him over the lip. It felt good to have solid ground under his feet again. Malcolm got on the radio and told Len to stand the *Molly Jane* down.

Bram pulled his helmet off and felt the wind and rain rummage through his fair hair, but he needed the air. He felt good. This was the kind of buzz that made volunteering worthwhile. Most of the rescues had happy endings. If only Regan could have seen that.

The paramedics had got Georgie into the ambulance out of the wind and they'd already hooked her up to a drip. They worked fast, those guys, but then they had to. The door shut and the vehicle sped away towards the road. Gone but not forgotten. Strange to think he'd probably never see the kid again, unless her mother took her down to the lifeboat station to thank the crew. And Len would probably pick her up and take her on a tour of the *Emerson Fitzgerald*, the Severn-class lifeboat they used for all weathers which was the pride and joy of the crew. There was also the smaller inshore boat, the *Molly Jane*, which would have been involved in the rescue tonight if things hadn't gone as well as they had. Georgie might even get a ride on it round the harbour.

'Great work, Bram!' Malcolm's hand came towards him upraised. He raised his hand in return and they slapped palms — and at that point everything went pear-shaped.

Bram felt the earth beneath his feet give way and then the drop, hard and fast, and Malcolm's bellow before he felt the rope he was still attached to pull taut, jerking his whole body and slapping him back against the rock face, blasting the air out of his body, and then . . . nothing.

2

'Someone didn't get enough sleep today,' Josie Howard laughed when she walked up to the desk and caught ENP Sister Regan Tyler halfway through a yawn.

Someone didn't get any sleep at all today, if the truth was known, Regan thought wryly. Thanks to the heating system breaking down at Oaks Drive School, her daughter had been sent home and Regan's sleep time had been seriously compromised. Bless her heart, Georgie had tried very hard to be quiet, but Regan couldn't sleep. A five-year-old needed supervision, not to mention company, and in the end she'd given up even trying to snatch a few winks. It was at times like this she found being a single parent hardest. How nice it would be to have someone say, 'Get off to bed, love. You look all in. I'll keep an eye on Georgie.' But there was only one someone she'd want to say that to her, and that was a scenario so far out of the question it was way over the other side of the planet. Georgie's father was long gone from her life and he wasn't coming back.

Regan didn't mind working nights, but it wasn't an easy shift when you had a five-year-old daughter — a very lively daughter at that. Lally Shires stayed over to look after Georgie when Regan worked the night shift. She was a good neighbour, a nice woman and a real friend.

She picked up the records of the next patient waiting in Minors and gave Josie a grin. 'Stanley Bishop again — I wonder what it is this time?'

'Poor old guy,' Josie said, screwing her face up. 'But I'm glad he's yours.'

'Ah, he says it's his heart,' Regan sighed as she checked the admission card. 'But I guess it probably has more to do with this heavy rain. I daresay sleeping under the arches gets pretty damp in this weather.'

'We're not a homeless shelter, Regan,' Josie said, but her pretty grey eyes weren't without sympathy. There was something gentle and harmless about old Stanley and if coming in here got him out of the wind and the rain for a little while, then who was to know? If Minors happened to be busy on a night that Stanley came in, then he was left in chairs to wait the night out and often left the department when the sun came up and before the day shift arrived. If he happened to call in on an extremely busy night, then he slipped quietly away again, especially if Mike Anson, the department head, was about.

'I just hope he hasn't brought any visitors with him.' Josie grinned. 'Or you won't get any sleep tomorrow because you'll be scratching your bites!'

Regan rolled her eyes. It wouldn't be the first time. 'That'll be your ambulance arriving,' she said as sirens approached. 'What have we got coming in?'

'A child went over the cliffs and

thank goodness someone saw her and reported it. They found her on a ledge near the bottom, but I gather her injuries aren't life-threatening.'

Regan shook her head. Kids could be daft sometimes. She wouldn't mind betting the child was a teenager who'd been playing a game of dare with her mates, probably showing off in front of some lads. Those kinds of accidents usually involved locals who should know better and should certainly have more respect for the area in which they lived — not to mention respect for themselves.

'Right, Stanley.' She looked up from the notes and smiled at the empty chairs and the one grey-coated and rather wet figure sitting slap-bang in the middle.

He looked up, surprised, his eyebrows rising slightly. 'Oh, is it my turn?' he asked breathlessly. It was a game they played. He always pretended to be pleasantly surprised and since he was only called if they weren't busy, it was a game they were happy to indulge. The longer it took him to walk from the chairs to the cubicle, the longer he would be inside and out of the rain. It wasn't right that an old person should have to live like that, Regan thought, but she had no idea why he lived the life he did. Perhaps it was through choice. It seemed sad that at his age there was no one to take proper care of him — no warm-hearted daughter to take him shopping, no strapping grandson to do a bit of decorating for him.

She held his arm as they walked through. He was amazingly thin beneath the layers of wet clothing. They'd offered to try and get him 'in' somewhere, but he wasn't having any of that. He'd rather end his days on the ground under a flattened cardboard box than imprisoned in a home. That was how he saw it: prison.

The doors opened and the paramedics came in with the cliff-fall casualty. Funny, but the figure on the bed didn't look much like a teenager. In fact she looked rather small. Not that Regan could see much. The paramedics were rapping out what had happened as they sped towards Resus with Josie and the duty doctor, Karen, running alongside.

Regan's eyes strayed to the doors, waiting for them to open, for an anxious parent or two to come through. No one came. And now the phone was ringing and everyone else was busy.

'Excuse me,' Regan said, sitting Stanley on a chair inside an empty cubicle. 'I'll just get that. I'll be right back.'

'Take your time, dear.' Stanley smiled. 'I'm in no hurry. In fact my heart feels a lot better since I got here.'

The call was brief. Regan hung up and hurried over to Resus. The door opened and Josie came out, her face as white as a sheet.

'There's another ambulance on the way,' Regan said, watching Josie carefully. 'Apparently the lifeboat guy who retrieved the casualty then went over the cliff himself. Suspected spinal injuries. Would . . . What's the matter, Josie? You look as if you've seen a ghost. You haven't lost her?'

'Sorry, there's no easy way to say this. It's Georgie,' Josie said, reaching out and touching Regan's arm.

Regan blinked, confused. What did she mean? Georgie was at home in bed.

'Georgie was the child that went over the cliff,' Josie went on, her voice leaden because she knew the impact the news would have on Regan. 'She's okay, she's not badly hurt, but . . . '

'Georgie?' Regan whispered. Her heart felt as if it had dropped like a stone right down through her chest into the pit of her stomach. She felt her insides tighten, her heart freeze with fear. 'My Georgie? No way. You must be mistaken, Josie.'

'No mistake I'm afraid, Regan. Go in with her,' Josie said, smiling but looking as if she might be about to burst into tears herself. 'But be prepared. She's got a scalp injury so there's quite a lot of blood. I know you're used to it, but when it's your own . . . '

The lead in Regan's feet turned to air and she flew through the door and into Resus, where she saw her own little girl on the bed, her head immobilised in a brace while Karen gently checked out her arm.

'Mummy!' Georgie wailed.

'Oh, sweetheart, what have you done?' Regan said, rushing to her daughter's side and taking her uninjured hand in hers. Her eyes looked very bright against the mask of red covering her face. Even her little hands were scarlet with blood.

'I fell off the cliff, Mummy,' Georgie said, and at that point it all became too much for her and she burst into tears, relief at seeing her mother tipping her off the fine brave line she'd been treading.

This was not the time to ask why she had been on the cliff. That could wait. Right now Regan needed to know the extent of her injuries. She looked at Karen.

'She's going to be okay, Regan,'

Karen said. 'Has she any allergies we should know about? Regan?'

'Yes? Er, no,' Regan said, pulling herself together. 'She's fine with anything.' She squeezed Georgie's hand and felt another hand squeeze round her heart. She'd always been good at what ifs — too good — and now the what ifs were coming thick and fast. What if no one had seen her go over the side? What if she'd missed that ledge?

She felt as if she was a still picture in one of those films where everyone else moves at super speed. Everything happened so fast around them, yet in the middle of it all, Regan stood beside the bed holding Georgie's hand, her mind crowded with thoughts. She left briefly to call Lally and let her know, but it sounded as if Lally had just found an empty bed anyway and was already upset and sobbing.

When she got back, Mike Anson, their department head, had arrived. 'What are you doing here, Mike?' Regan asked, instantly worried. Why had Karen called in reinforcements?

'I've been visiting my father,' Mike explained. 'He's in Baker Ward. I heard about the incident on the cliffs and that there's the possibility of more casualties, so I thought I'd swing by and see if I could help.' He reached out and squeezed Regan's shoulder.

Regan thought briefly of Stanley waiting in the cubicle. If Mike knew he was here cluttering up his department — even if it was empty — he'd do his nut! Then she thought of Georgie, the focus of all this attention. She could have been killed this evening. Mike could have been down here comforting her for completely different reasons.

She blamed Bram for this. Bram and his reckless genes. Only a child of his would venture too close to the edge of a cliff when she shouldn't have been there in the first place. Not content with inheriting his vivid blue eyes and the dark lashes that went with them, she'd taken on his outgoing personality. Regan couldn't look at her daughter without being reminded of Bram and she'd learned to live with that, but how was she going to live with another daredevil?

'Don't cry, Mummy,' Georgie said.

'I'm not crying.' Regan forced a laugh and rubbed at her eyes. 'Silly old thing! I'm just tired.' Golden rule for parents with kids in hospital — You do not cry in front of them and make them even more frightened than they already are. You smile, you don't look worried and you speak with utter conviction that everything is going to be all right. Which it is!

'I'm going to take Georgie into theatre now, Regan,' Mike told her. 'I'll get that arm sorted out, make her comfortable, and she should be able to come home in a day or two. Did you want to be with her while we put her under?'

'Stay with me, Mummy,' Georgie pleaded, her voice so small and helpless it nearly tore Regan's heart out. 'Don't go. Stay.'

'Of course I'll stay with you, darling,' Regan said. It would be just until she was put under, then Regan would slip away, ready to return when Georgie was in recovery so she'd be there beside her when she woke up.

And it was only after Georgie's eyes had closed and Regan was no longer needed that she allowed the tears to come.

'She'll be all right, Regan,' Mike said, his eyes serious over the top of his mask. 'She's safe in my hands.'

'I know,' she whispered. 'But she's my little girl.'

As she hurried back to A&E, she wondered what on earth Georgie thought she was doing tonight. And she had to try to figure out some way of curbing her daughter's wild streak.

'I tell you I'm fine!' The voice stopped Regan dead in her tracks. That voice! No mistaking it. She shook her head and carried on. Tiredness and worry were making her delusional. She'd been thinking rather too much about Bram tonight, that was all. There was no way he was here in her hospital, no way on earth. When she'd sent him away, he'd gone for good and he'd been most adamant he wouldn't be coming back.

Way back then he'd looked up at her from his wheelchair, his bruised, battered and stitched face changed almost beyond recognition. He'd looked far from beautiful, but it wasn't his beauty she'd fallen in love with. If he'd had a face like the back of a bus she would still have been in love with him and the scars and bruises made no difference to how she felt about him. If anything they made her love him more, which made it hurt even more, and it was a pain she just couldn't bear.

They were just back from their friend Tom's funeral, still in their black clothing. Regan had brought Bram back to the hospital to continue his treatment and the funeral had exhausted him. Regan could not get the image of Tom's widow at the graveside out of her mind. She stood erect and pale, flanked by her two white-faced weeping children as they watched their hero being lowered into the ground. Their dead hero. Regan didn't want a dead hero — she wanted a living, breathing man in her life. Bram had almost died and as well as his physical injuries from the sea rescue that had gone so dreadfully wrong, he had psychological scars that would never heal. He'd kept Tom afloat, struggled to keep him above water, but Tom had already been dead and Bram almost lost his own life hanging on to a corpse.

'If I walk out that door, Regan, it's the last you'll see of me, I promise you that.'

'Fine,' she'd said hotly. 'Then hurry up and go. I can't wait.'

He hadn't walked and he wasn't going anywhere but back to the ward. What he had actually done was to spin his wheelchair around and wheel himself towards the door, battering at the sensor switch until it opened; then it had shut softly behind him and the steady squeak of his wheels had been silenced. She'd wanted to run after him, grab the handles of the chair and turn it round, but what would be the point? He'd said as soon as he was recovered he'd be back on duty on the lifeboats, and she'd told him to choose. She'd given him her ultimatum, fired up by grief and fear. Just be a vet, she'd said — be content to save the lives of dogs and cats; give up the RNLI, the rescues, the danger. Give it up or go.

'If you knew anything about me, Regan,' he'd said, 'you'd never demand I make a choice like that.'

'And if you really loved me there would be no choice to make.'

'I could say the same thing,' he'd said sadly.

And he had made his choice. When she swallowed her pride and went to see him at the hospital a few days later, he'd gone and no one seemed to know where. But he was wrong about her not seeing him again. She saw him every day in the face of their little girl.

The voice crashed into her thoughts again. 'This is just a waste of time — it's just a bit of bruising! I've had a bruised spine and believe me, this is not it! This is minor. Just let me go home, love, eh?'

Regan turned round and took a step towards Resus, where Josie was standing at the open door looking out at her, her face a mask of anguish as if she couldn't stand any more shocks. It couldn't be, Regan thought, even though her ears and Josie's expression were telling her otherwise. No way. He'd gone. He'd promised not to come back.

'First of all, I'm the doctor here and I will decide whether or not your injuries are minor,' Karen said patiently. 'And I am not your love!'

Regan would have laughed if the patient had been anyone else being put in his place. But Bram, here? Impossible!

3

'Hey, how's Georgie?' Josie said, trying to head her off. Josie would remember Bram of course; remember that once upon a time he and Regan had actually meant something to each other.

Regan took another step towards Resus.

'Regan, don't go in there . . . '

'Look, I'll leave you to yourself for a minute,' Karen said, exasperation making her voice tight. 'Just think about being co-operative and making things easier for everyone concerned. I'll be back.'

'When you do, bring those discharge papers for me to sign — I don't intend to spend the rest of the night here.'

Karen emerged from Resus, cheeks bright pink. 'Would you believe that guy?' she said, throwing her hands up in the air. 'Talk about stubborn!'

'But very good-looking.' Josie grinned

and Regan shot her a warning look. Karen was a relative newcomer, as were most of the Accident and Emergency staff at the new hospital. Regan's former relationship with Bram wasn't exactly common knowledge, and she wanted it to stay that way.

Bram's time in Walsea had been almost as brief as their relationship. He'd come to the town a newly qualified young vet on a year's contract to work with Dennis, who owned the only veterinary practice in town. He'd left three months before the end of his contract, taking Regan's heart with him. He had no roots here, no reason to come back — so what the hell was he doing back?

'That too,' Karen admitted, and Regan realised the flush in her cheeks had nothing to do with her being cross, but everything to do with her being attracted. Well nothing had changed in that department then. Bram was still attracting women like wasps round a jam pot. He made a big impact on the town last time he was here and there was no reason to suppose this time would be any different.

'I'll talk to him,' Regan said, setting her shoulders straight and taking in a deep breath.

'You will?' Karen said, surprised. 'What about Georgie?'

'Mike's operating,' Regan explained. 'I won't be needed for a while.'

'Well good luck,' Karen said. 'Let me know when you've tamed him.'

Tamed him? Oh, no one would ever do that. Regan walked in and let the door close behind her. She looked around. The boards on the wall were smothered in notices and memos, and the desk was the same. It was never like that on television. Things were always so much neater and more orderly on television, at least where paperwork was concerned.

There were two beds with curtains between them. Bram was in the one at the far end. Regan's heart gave a thud and she almost gasped. All she could see of him around the half-pulled curtain was a pair of tanned, muscular shins and two large feet.

She took another step closer, and another. More of him came into view, but he was half-covered with a sheet, lying flat on his back, arms at his sides . . . She edged closer . . . His face was turned away from her, staring at a raft of equipment to his side. The sight of that fair tousled hair on the pillow made her knees buckle. She must have made some sound because he turned his head slowly and his eyes widened in surprise.

He sat up. 'Regan . . . Regan? Is that you? My God, it is you!' And his face broke into the most wondrous smile of recognition as if he were really, truly pleased to see her. His eyes had practically ignited and his smile didn't waver. Had whatever happened to him out there on the cliff wiped out his memory? Taken him back to a time when they were happy together? 'It's so good to see you.'

'Is it?' she asked coolly. She picked up her pace and hurried to his bedside, picking up his notes simply to give herself something to do, not looking at him. Oh God, no, she couldn't look at him; couldn't let herself fall into those summer-ocean-blue eyes and let herself drown all over again. It had hurt too much last time. It still did.

'You rescued the little girl?' she said as everything suddenly fell into place and she realised why he was here. 'It was you that saved Georgie? You're back with the RNLI?' She looked at him, then looked away again. It was Bram who had rescued Georgie. She could scarcely breathe, and for one awful dizzying moment, Regan thought that she was going to faint.

'I've always been a volunteer, Regan,' he said, and she knew he was staring at her; she could feel his eyes burning into her. 'I was before I met you and I've never stopped. You know that. Nothing's changed.'

'I should th . . . thank you for what

you did,' she said, still staring at the notes, her heart pumping like a piston engine. *Thank him, yes, but for God's sake don't tell him why! Tread carefully here, Regan; don't let what's happened make you blurt something out you will later regret.*

'Maybe her mother should be doing that,' he said, anger giving his voice a raw edge. 'Poor little scrap, left to wander the cliffs on her own. Don't these people realise kids are a gift to be treasured?'

Oh, get him started on kids! It was his pet subject. Children and animals, helpless and vulnerable and unable a lot of the time to take care of themselves. If he hadn't been a vet, he'd have been a paediatrician, and a damn good one too.

'Hey, Regan,' he called softly, and she was reminded of just how persuasive he could be. 'You can swing it for me to go home, can't you? You know how I hate hospitals, and there's no one at home with the dogs, and I've got surgery

36

starting at eight tomorrow.'

'Surgery?' Her eyes snapped up, met his head-on, and crashed spectacularly. Still so blue, still so beautiful. 'You mean you're in practice around here again?' She hoped he'd say he was just doing locum work for Dennis, just here for a couple of weeks.

He stared at her for a moment, a faint flush rising in his cheeks. He'd changed — and it wasn't just the faint scar running down the side of his face, so dangerously close to his eye. Considering the mess he'd been in last time she'd seen him, he looked pretty good now. Better than good.

'I bought Dennis out when he retired,' he said, having the grace to look at least a little uncomfortable that he'd made such a big move without informing her. 'I know I'm the last person you want in town, Regan, but it's a big enough place and there's no reason our paths should ever cross. I liked my time here and I've always kept in touch with Dennis, so when he told me he was retiring, well I jumped at the chance to come back to be honest.'

She had no idea Dennis had retired or that his practice was in new hands. She didn't even know he'd kept in touch with Bram, presumably at Bram's request. Her face burned. How many times had she been to the surgery with Bonnie her dog and taken Georgie along? How many times must Dennis have looked at the child and seen Bram? Had he said anything?

'Hell, Regan.' Bram's voice cracked. 'It's not so terrible me being back here, is it? You don't still hate me that much, do you?'

'Hate you? I never ... How long have you been back?'

'A month,' he muttered. Then he lifted one side of his mouth in a crooked grin. 'You really don't hate me?'

'You know I don't. But you've only been here a month and here we are, crossing paths already. Did you really think you could just come back and pick up your life again and not expect to bump into me? Or did you come back for just that purpose?'

'I didn't come back here to see you, Regan,' he said quietly. 'But I must admit I'm not sorry that I have.'

'Then why?' Her heart was hammering.

'I like it here.' He shrugged. 'It's the first place in my whole life that ever felt like home.'

She threw his notes down, anger bubbling up inside her. How dare he come back now? How dare he break his promise that she would never have to see him again? Didn't he have any idea how much it hurt?

'Regan,' he said, the gentleness of his voice slicing chunks out of her. 'It's been six years. I thought maybe you'd moved on by now. I certainly hope you have.' Six years. Then why did it suddenly feel like six minutes? Six minutes since he went away and her life came crumbling down. Six minutes since he turned his stubborn back and left her. But she'd moved on all right.

He had no idea just how much she'd moved on.

'Discharge yourself, Bram,' she said, all brisk efficiency and not a hint of the turmoil inside. 'I'll get Karen to bring you the form to sign yourself out of here. Your scan was clear, but you know what to look out for. Come back if you have any reason to worry.'

'Thanks.' He winked at her and scrambled her insides.

'Yes, well — Thank me once you're in the clear. If you collapse and die ten minutes after you get home, don't come complaining to me.'

'I won't.' He grinned.

She smiled. Despite everything, she smiled. Couldn't help herself. She left on shaky legs and stopped outside to get her breath back. He hadn't seemed at all fazed to see her. In fact, she might just have been any other face from his past. Was that all she was to him — a reminder of the past? Probably, she decided, he obviously didn't think they had been that important or he wouldn't have come back. And she could excuse him that because after all, he didn't have the daily reminder of their child to keep the memories fresh.

'Well?' Karen asked when she emerged from Resus. 'Did you work your usual magic?'

'He needs a discharge form,' Regan said stiffly. 'And probably a taxi.' But then she saw Len waiting, legs sprawled out, head back, eyes closed. 'Maybe not the taxi. It seems his ride home is covered.'

'Does he realise..?' Karen began.

'He knows the score,' Regan said. She checked her watch. Still a while to go before she had to be back with Georgie.

'You sound as if you know him,' Karen said, unsettling Regan with the intensity of her gaze.

'I know a lost cause when I see one,' Regan replied airily, and made her way over to the lifeboat man. 'Hey, Len,' she said, shaking the big man's shoulder. 'Len. Wake up.'

'What? Hey! Regan!' He grinned up

at her, then the grin faded and he chewed on his lower lip. 'Regan . . . Oh heck.'

'You didn't tell me he was back, Len,' she said accusingly.

'I didn't?'

'You were in here less than a week ago when I stitched your hand. How long did that take? How long were we talking?' She looked towards the ceiling. 'Let me see, you told me about your nephew's new quad bike and how good the fishing's been this year and how you'd had to get the brakes fixed on your Toyota, but at no point did you think to mention that my ex was back in town.'

'I meant to,' he said, swallowing hard. 'I just . . . I was waiting for the right time and it never seemed to come up and besides, it all happened years ago, and . . . You know people have short memories. I thought maybe if nothing was said that you and he might . . . '

'You're not making any sense at all, Len,' she said. 'Are you sure you didn't bash your head too?' She didn't see much of Len, but he knew about Georgie and although she'd never confirmed it to anyone, everyone that knew she and Bram must have figured it out pretty quickly. It was only a matter of time till Bram found out the truth.

'I seem to remember telling you the lifeboat was out of bounds for a fortnight, Len. At least until the stitches were out — which they aren't,' she added. 'What is it with you guys? You risk your necks saving other people, but won't take care of yourselves.'

'Are you talking about me now — or are you still talking about Bram?' Len asked sheepishly.

'He'll be ready to go home in a minute,' she said wearily, damping down her anger. No use taking it out on Len. Poor guy. It wasn't his fault. 'Keep an eye on him though, Len.'

'Yeah, sure.' He ran his hand through his spiky grey hair. 'Regan, it has to be done, love. If it weren't for people like us — like Bram, willing to take a little risk — then people would die. That little girl might have died. I didn't want him going over that cliff tonight, but there was no other way. We could have waited for the fire brigade, but they were out in force attending a massive chemical leak. And a big wave could have had her in the oggin if Bram hadn't got to her when he did.'

Oh the irony of that! Her child — their child — might have died if not for Bram doing the very job she'd begged him to give up.

'At least he wasn't out on the water with the rest of us,' Len added as if that would make the slightest difference.

Regan shook her head. She knew she had been unreasonable six years ago, but she'd acted purely out of fear — fear of losing him, and she'd lost him anyway. If she had that time back, would she do things differently? Probably. But could she have lived with that gnawing fear that she might lose him in the most tragic of circumstances, especially once they had a child?

'I have to go,' she said. 'Good night, Len.'

'Any luck tracing the kid's mother?'

'Why is it always the mother with you guys, huh?' she said. 'Never the father.' She walked away from him, shaking her head just as the doors were flung open and Lally Shires rushed in, straight over to Regan, where she burst into tears.

Len looked about ready to say something, so Regan led Lally away, well away. She didn't want to be anywhere near Len or Bram — not tonight, not ever, not after this.

'She's all right, Lally,' Regan said. 'Broke her arm, gashed her head, but she's okay.'

'But you're not okay! I can see you've been crying.' Lally wept, clutching at Regan's hand. Her shoulder-length grey hair was like a cloud around her face. 'I'm so sorry, Regan. I swear I didn't know she'd gone out.'

'Of course you didn't.' Regan smiled, rubbing Lally's back as she spoke. True she'd been as mad as hell at first, but there was no point apportioning blame now. It wouldn't change anything. 'If you knew, you'd have stopped her.'

'I dozed off for a while after she went to bed,' Lally explained. 'Then when I woke up, I made myself a coffee and then I realised Bonnie wasn't around. Is Georgie really going to be all right, Regan?'

Okay, now more alarm bells were ringing. 'What about Bonnie, Lally? Did you find her?'

'I checked she wasn't outside, then I thought maybe she'd gone up and climbed on Georgie's bed, and that's when I realised Georgie had gone . . . Well not straight away, because I checked the bathroom, and then the phone rang and it was you, and . . . Oh, Regan, I'm so, so sorry. If that dear little girl had died because of me . . . '

Regan gritted her teeth. 'Lally, what about Bonnie?'

'Bonnie?' Lally looked at her through a blur of tears. 'I don't know. She must have gone out when Georgie did. Oh,

Regan, you don't think . . . ?'

Regan didn't have time to think. She ran back to reception in time to see Len and Bram disappearing out the door, Bram walking with that stiff, hurt gait she'd seen so often before.

Bonnie was still out there somewhere. What if she'd gone over the cliff too? She was a clever dog — no, calling her clever was an injustice. She was more than clever. She was perceptive and loving, and she hadn't a mean bone in her body. If it hadn't been for Bonnie, there were plenty of times Regan might have fallen apart. She sprinted for the doors.

'Len!' she shouted as the doors opened and the wind blasted cold rain into her face. 'Bram!'

'I'm not changing my mind, Regan,' Bram said, turning and looking at her through silver needles pounding down from the sky. 'I'm not readmitting myself under any circumstances.'

'My dog,' she croaked. 'Georgie's dog . . . '

Both men looked at each other, then back at Regan. Neither had heard her correctly, but at least she'd got their attention.

'Did you say something about a dog, Regan?' Bram said. 'Where? What?' He was walking back towards her. He looked so big and tough, but a lot of that was the jacket, wasn't it? He towered over her. How could she have forgotten how tall he was? How big and strong and indestructible. Yet she knew only too well that he wasn't indestructible. He was flesh and blood and as vulnerable as any other human being. She looked up at him, hoping her tears would mingle with the rain and become invisible. Could this night get any worse?

'What dog, Regan?'

'Georgie's dog,' she said, licking rain from her lips and blinking it out of her eyelashes. 'She's a black-and-white Springer spaniel, same age as Georgie — they grew up together. She's still out there somewhere. You have to find her, Bram.'

'Get back inside, Regan,' Bram said, clamping a wet hand on her shoulder and squeezing gently. 'You're getting soaked and your patients won't appreciate you dripping all over them. We'll do a search for the dog — what did you say her name was?'

'I didn't,' Regan said. 'It's Bonnie.'

'We'll find her,' Bram said in a tone that left her in no doubt that he would.

'A dog missing, you say?' Len had come back to join them and caught the tail end of the conversation. 'I'll find her, Bram. You're going home. Doctor's orders. I'll rustle up some of the lads and we'll do a search. Tell the little girl not to worry, Regan — we'll find her dog for her. Did I hear you right? Did you say it was Georgie in there? And isn't Bonnie your..?'

She flashed him a look and shook her head, and Len's lips tightened. He'd obviously heard more than she realised. Bram was already walking away.

'Georgie?' Len whispered. 'Jesus!'

'Don't say anything to him, Len. Not

until I've had a chance to talk to him.'

Len nodded and squeezed her arm. 'We'll find her, love,' he said.

She hurried back inside and Karen waved her through. 'Go on up to be with Georgie,' she said. 'We'll manage down here. Come back once she's settled for the night, okay?'

'Thanks, Karen.'

'You okay?'

Regan nodded, but she couldn't get Bonnie out of her mind. What if she was lying injured somewhere? The thought of that sweet dog in pain and afraid was more than she could bear. But she had to hide those feelings, push them back and keep them away; otherwise Georgie, no matter how drowsy she was after the operation, would see right through her.

4

'It makes sense,' Bram said as he strode up the hill towards the cliff, ignoring Len's protests and the pain in his back. The pain relief they'd given him at the hospital had started to kick in and he was walking more easily. 'I'm a vet. If you find the dog and it's hurt, which it most probably will be, you're going to need me here.' They were forming a line along the edge, torchlight beams flashing in the darkness, lighting up the rods of driving rain.

'Don't try to kid me,' Len said. 'This has nothing to do with the dog and everything to do with Regan.'

Regan's face flashed into Bram's mind. Not the face that had haunted him for the past six years — that pretty young elfin face with its frame of closely cropped dark hair — but the face that had looked at him tonight through the splintery rain.

She'd changed. Boy how she'd changed. Her face was still pretty, but her hair was longer now — long enough to be tied back in a dark ponytail, and her cheekbones seemed more defined. If anything she was more beautiful than he remembered; her lips seemed fuller, her eyes darker and deeper, as if something more was hidden behind them. She looked as if she'd been crying, but why? Because of him? No — she'd been surprised to see him, but not upset enough to cry. He couldn't define what the difference was, just that there seemed to be more to Regan than there was before, much more.

But then, six years was a long time. She could be married by now. She could have kids. That would explain her rounder figure. He could just see her surrounded by little miniature Regans — in fact that was how he used to see her, except in those days there had been miniature Brams there too. They'd talked about having kids — loads of kids.

'It has nothing to do with Regan,' Bram said firmly. 'Believe me — Regan and I were finished a long time ago. It's the dog that concerns me, Len.'

The guys were shouting the dog's name, but if she'd gone over the cliff there wasn't much hope for her. How did a kid and her dog come to be wandering about on the cliff at night? Bram wondered again. It would be up to the medical staff at the hospital whether to involve social services, but it was something that should be investigated.

He turned his thoughts to the dog. Springers were pretty robust dogs: plenty of stamina and pretty smart too, despite their scatty reputation. If she had got herself into some kind of hole, she'd probably be trying to get herself out of it. He cupped his hands round his mouth and joined in the shouting, but he still didn't hold out much hope, not if she'd gone over the side. And that sweet little girl would have to learn to cope with losing her best friend, possibly her only friend on top of everything else.

* ★ ★

Georgie was awake and thankfully not in pain. She had a plaster cast on her arm and a neat row of six stitches on her scalp. Considering what she'd been through, she was remarkably cheerful, but then she always had been a resilient child. She took after Bram in her ability to bounce back.

'You're going to need to get back to sleep,' Regan said after sitting with her for a while. 'And I have to finish my shift. I'll come back and have breakfast with you, okay? Oh, and by the way . . .'

She hesitated. She'd been worried about how to bring up the subject of Bonnie without upsetting Georgie. There were plenty of other questions to be asked, like what on earth she was doing creeping out at night like that for a start, and why go to the cliffs? But right now there was just one question that needed urgently to be asked.

'Yes?' Georgie looked up at her, eyes still heavy.

'Did Bonnie go with you this evening?'

A flash of fear passed through Georgie's eyes, but tiredness was taking over.

'Georgie?'

'Yes,' Georgie said sleepily, her little mouth framing a yawn. 'But I told her to go home. I didn't want her to get hurt.'

'Then you realised what you were doing was dangerous?' Regan whispered.

'I didn't mean to fall, Mummy.' Georgie's eyes grew heavy.

Regan leaned over and kissed her forehead. 'Night night, darling,' she whispered. 'I'll see you later.'

She stood beside the bed looking down at her sleeping daughter. 'There's something else, Georgie Tyler,' she whispered. 'Something you're not telling me. What is it?' She hadn't a clue what it could be, but it worried her.

Back in the department, Josie met

Regan with a big smile on her face. 'You'll never guess what I found,' she said, pulling back a curtain. There was Stanley, sprawled out on the bed fast asleep, still wrapped in his wet raincoat.

'Oh, lord, I forgot all about him,' Regan said. 'Has Mike definitely gone?'

'Yes, don't worry,' Josie laughed. 'As soon as he'd finished with Georgie he left the hospital. What do you want me to do about Stanley?'

'Leave him to sleep,' Regan said. 'I'll wake him an hour or so before the day shift arrives and give him a quick check-over, then we'll send him over to Larry's with enough money for a cup of tea and a bacon sandwich for his breakfast. He'll be long gone by the time Mike comes back on duty. I don't suppose anyone has called about Bonnie?'

'By anyone, you mean Bram,' Josie said. 'No, I'm sorry, there's no news. But no news is good news, Regan.'

Regan wasn't so sure. She bit hard on her lip. It was bad enough knowing what Georgie had been through, but at least now she was safe and still in one piece. She was terrified that somewhere out there on this wild, stormy night, Bonnie was alone and frightened and suffering. The dog had a terror of thunderstorms, fireworks, and other loud noises. The roaring wind would be absolutely terrifying for her.

'I bet it was weird seeing him again,' Josie said. 'I mean it felt pretty strange for me, but you were practically engaged to the guy, and he's Georgie's father.'

'Don't say it!' Regan cried. 'Someone might hear.'

'But don't you think it's kind of spooky? I mean, him being there to save Georgie. He'd have held her in his arms and not even realised he was holding his own child.' Josie's face took on a dreamy expression, as if it was a wonderful thing that had happened — a reunion between father and daughter, with both unaware that it was happening.

'That's enough, Josie,' Regan said sharply, then smiled to take the edge off her words. 'I'm sorry, but I don't want to complicate matters. Bram mustn't find out.'

Josie shook her head. 'Oh, Regan,' she said. 'Of course he's going to find out. Sooner or later he's going to bump into someone who knows you both and he's going to be told — and then what? As for complicating matters, didn't you do that when you found out you were pregnant and chose not to let him know?'

Regan sighed. She knew how it must have appeared to other people — even to Josie, who probably knew her better than anyone. She didn't choose not to let Bram know, not as cold-bloodedly as that. In the first place, she hadn't known she was pregnant when she told him to go; and by the time she did, it was too late: he'd gone, and she didn't know how to find him.

True, she could have tracked him down if she'd tried hard enough, but how would that have looked? To have sent him away and then suddenly gone chasing after him when she found she was pregnant? Which led on to her second reason: the fact that she didn't want to be standing with her little girl at some cold graveside someday watching Bram being lowered into the ground in a box.

'Down there!' Len shouted, his torch beam shivering on the sand below. 'There's a dog. It must be her.'

Bram looked over the edge. The cliff had dropped away to grassy banks here, but they were pretty sheer. The dog had probably seen Georgie go over and had found herself an easier way down. Right now she was ignoring the men standing a few feet above her and was trying to pick her way over gigantic boulders on the beach. The tide had turned and was on the way out now so was no longer crashing murderously against the rocks, but still Bonnie was in a dangerous situation. One slip and she could trap her legs between the rocks.

Springers could be crazy, loopy, wilful dogs, but they were usually pretty obedient. And smart, despite their reputation.

The body language of this one said she was scared out of her wits, but determined to carry on.

'Bonnie!' Bram shouted. 'Wait!'

She stopped pawing at the rocks and looked round and up.

'Wait!' Bram repeated the command, hoping it was one she knew and understood. 'Good girl.'

Ha, she knew that all right. Her tail began to wag and she redoubled her efforts to get across the rocks. She was almost frantic now. It was as if she saw them as reinforcements and wanted them to join in the search.

'Where are you going?' Len said, grasping Bram's sleeve as he slid towards the slope.

'Where do you think, Len?' He grinned.

'No way. You slide down there and you could do yourself no end of damage. We'll get one of the other guys to go after her. Bram! Bram, do you ever listen to anything anyone says to you?'

'Sorry, Len,' Bram called over his shoulder. 'Can't hear you.'

He was at the edge of the grass preparing to drop himself down onto the beach. He landed, one foot hitting a jutting rock and wrenching over to the side. Biting back a yelp of pain, he turned to look at Bonnie. She was watching him, cautious and curious, her eyes flashing in the beam of Len's torch.

'Hey, girl,' he said softly. 'Come here. Come on.'

She lowered her head and wagged her tail some more, but didn't move.

'Come on, baby girl,' he said, squatting down and making himself as small and unthreatening as possible. She was soaking wet. God knew how long she'd been down here trying to make her way round the base of the cliff. She may even have tried to swim in the treacherous sea.

'I won't hurt you, Bonnie,' he said, holding out his hand to her. 'Come on. Come here. Come on, good girl.'

Squatting in this position wasn't doing a lot for his sore back or his wrenched ankle, but if he suddenly stood up he might scare her, and then she might make a bolt for it and really hurt herself.

Persistence and patience. Knowing her name helped. It was a word she recognised. A word used by those she loved and trusted. Bram repeated it over and over, calling her softly, his arm going stiff from holding it out to her. At last she took a step towards him, paws slipping and sliding on the rocks, tail still moving from side to side, although it was more of an uncertain wag rather than an 'Oh boy am I pleased to see you!' full-on wag. She had a rope round her neck, trailing along behind her. It was practically a noose and if it had got caught, it could have killed her.

'Good girl,' Bram said, his enthusiasm causing a real swing in her tail and a lifting of her ears. 'Good girl, Bonnie.'

She edged towards him, low and slow. The poor dog must have been through hell tonight. First she'd lost her little mistress, then she'd probably been scared out of her wits by all the rescue vehicles, lights and noise. Now here she was with this hard, slippery surface under her paws, freezing cold, soaked to the skin and not sure what was happening.

Bram knew if he made a grab for her, she'd probably turn tail and run — and run herself straight into danger and injury. He had to sit this out for as long as it took. Then he'd get her back to the surgery, check her out and report back to the hospital — to Regan, who could pass on the news that Bonnie was safe. Or he could let Len go back to the hospital with the news. That would be the sensible thing to do. But since when had he been sensible when it came to Regan? He wanted an excuse to see her again, though why he didn't know, because she made it pretty clear six years ago that she didn't really love him.

But then again, he hadn't put up much of a fight for her, had he? And he'd had his own reasons for wanting to get away. She'd played right into his hands and made breaking up easy.

On second thought, he'd leave the reporting back to Len. Safer that way. If Regan had made a new life for herself, he had no right to disrupt it.

Bonnie braced herself and shook, spraying him with cold, gritty water. 'Come on, girl,' he urged, and she took those last couple of steps closer. As he reached to grab her collar, she launched herself into his arms, knocking him backwards. He held on to her and ran his fingers through the thick curls on her chest, which were sodden and sticky with sand and saltwater. Now she'd decided to trust him, Bonnie went crazy and her pink tongue shot out again and again, slapping Bram around the face and making him laugh.

At last he managed to stand up, scoop the dog into his arms and carry her over to the bank. 'Let the hospital know we've found her,' he called up to Len.

'Already done,' Len said. 'Is she okay? She looks okay.'

'She seems fine as far as I can tell, but I'll take her back to the surgery, wash the sand and salt out of her fur and check her over to be sure.'

Len watched Bram hurry away with the dog in his arms. Regan's dog! The guy should be told that he'd rescued his own daughter tonight, but it wasn't his place to tell him. Regan was terrified he'd find out. She'd asked him again not to say anything when he called her just now — once she'd finished crying with relief and he'd managed to convince her that Bonnie was okay.

'He won't hear it from me,' Len promised. 'But he will hear it from someone, Regan, and it'll be sooner rather than later. You owe it — '

'I don't owe him anything.'

'Don't you? He saved Georgie's life. No one else would have had the guts to do what he did, and if we'd waited for the proper support, it may have been too late.'

'I didn't mean . . . ' She sounded as if she was crying and he felt terrible, but he loved both these people, Bram and Regan, and he wanted what was best for them both. And for that little girl too. Bram's little girl.

Regan hadn't so much as looked at another guy since Bram left, and she'd been so determined to block out the past, she'd even distanced herself from old friends. He'd done his best to stay in touch and help when he could, but she was fiercely independent. The only person that seemed to get anywhere near was Lally. Nice woman. Kept herself to herself for the most part. She wasn't local. Maybe that was why Regan had let her in.

At first when Bram showed up back in town, Len thought he'd come back to be with Regan and that he knew about Georgie, but it had soon become clear that wasn't the case.

* * *

When it was time to go home, Regan saw Lally waiting for her. 'What are you doing still here?' she said. 'You should have gone home ages ago.'

'I'm going to drive you home, that's what,' Lally said. 'You can leave your car in the car park here. You didn't get much sleep yesterday and you've had a lousy night, so I don't think you should drive. That's all.'

'Lally, you don't have to . . . '

'I know I don't,' Lally interrupted. 'But if it was one of my kids and someone had let me down the way I let you down, I'd want to kill them. So if you want to hit me, go right ahead.' She jutted her chin out. It made Regan laugh. She'd no more think of hitting Lally than she would turn Stanley Bishop away on a cold and stormy night. She linked her arm through Lally's instead.

'You didn't let me down.'

'Well, I feel responsible.'

Lally had no children of her own and it was a pity, because she was the most motherly person Regan had ever met — and that included her own mother.

'I'm not going home, Lally,' she said. 'I'm going to pick Bonnie up from the vet, then I'm coming back here to be with Georgie.'

'Now you're being silly,' Lally said. 'You need to catch up on some sleep so you're wide awake later on. Georgie's going to need you. Bonnie will be fine at the surgery. They'll take good care of her and she'll probably just want to sleep anyway.'

Regan sighed and bit her lip, fighting back tears again when she thought of her lovely Bonnie. 'They said she was trying to find Georgie. That doesn't surprise me one little bit. She's such a lovely, loyal little dog. I should bring her home. I don't think I can sleep anyway after all that's happened.'

There was another reason she wanted to go to the surgery. She had to see Bram and get this all out in the open before it was too late. Strike while the iron was hot, wasn't that how the saying went? Well this iron was scalding!

'You have to try and sleep, Regan.

You're going to be no use to Georgie if you drop dead of exhaustion. I'll go and pick Bonnie up for you later.'

They were outside the hospital now. The rain had stopped and daylight glowed weakly through multi-coloured clouds. But still she hesitated. Would it be too cowardly of her to agree, to let Lally fetch Bonnie? She was too tired to be brave.

'Thank you. Make sure he gives you a bill. Tell him I'll settle up with him later.' It wasn't just the bill she needed to settle. She turned back to the hospital. 'I should stay . . . '

'All right, how about this,' Lally said. 'You get a taxi home and I'll stay here with Georgie. At least you won't have to worry about having to hurry back to the hospital. They're not expecting you to work tonight, are they?'

'No,' Regan said. 'I've taken some leave.' She knew it made sense to at least try and catch up. She needed to be able to think straight if she was going to sort things out with Bram.

'That's settled then,' Lally said firmly.

'All right,' Regan agreed. 'But promise you'll let me know if Georgie needs me?'

'Of course I will,' Lally said. 'When can she come home?'

'Tomorrow,' Regan said. 'They're keeping her in for another twenty-four hours and all being well, she'll be discharged.'

'Has she said what she was doing on the cliff?' Lally asked.

'Not yet,' Regan said. 'But I'm going to find out and I'll make sure she never does anything like it again.' Right now, Regan would like to wrap her daughter up in cotton wool and keep her at home and never let her out of her sight again.

'I don't think you need worry too much about that,' Lally said. 'After the fright she's had, she'll want to stay close to home for a while.'

'I hope you're right.'

Regan hugged Lally, then called a taxi firm. Despite her protestations, she

70

felt really tired, and it would be foolish to drive. But she was determined to be up again soon. A tear slid down her cheek and she rubbed it away. 'There's something else you should know, Lally,' Regan said while they waited for the taxi. 'About Bram.'

'The guy who rescued Georgie? He found Bonnie too, didn't he?'

Regan nodded. There was no easy way to say it, so she just came right out with it. 'He's Georgie's dad.'

'What?' Lally cried. 'But I thought her dad had moved away? You're a dark horse, Regan Tyler! When did he come back? Are you and he . . . ?'

Poor Lally. She looked so hopeful. Bless her, she was all about the happy endings.

'He doesn't know,' Regan said. 'He knows nothing about Georgie.'

Lally's jaw dropped. Her look of shock was almost funny, but the last thing Regan felt like was laughing.

'I never told you about him before because it was in the past and all happened before you moved here. I think that's why we've always got along so well. I knew you were never going to ask awkward questions.'

Lally shook her head. 'Daft lass,' she said. 'We get on well because we just do! I don't care about your past, but I am concerned about you now. He doesn't know, you say? Well he's going to find out for sure, isn't he? But you know me. I won't tell you what I think you should do, but I'll be there to support you whatever you decide. Okay? And don't ever keep anything from me because of what I might think or say or do. That's not what friendship is about, Regan.'

Regan hugged her and struggled to fight back more tears. What would she do without Lally? 'Bless you, my lovely friend,' she said. She really must get some sleep before she ended up a tear-sodden mess.

5

There were no overnight guests at the surgery, so the place was quiet. Bram let himself in and Bonnie followed through the door somewhat reluctantly. She must know exactly where she was as she seemed quite familiar with her surroundings.

He rinsed her fur with warm water, then dried her with towels and she shook again, still finding a fair bit of water in her fur to shower him with.

'That's no way to thank me for saving your life, Bonnie,' he laughed. She gazed up at him. How quickly they came to put their trust in you. It amazed him how even the most nervous of dogs would soon attach themselves to you if you showed them kindness.

He gave her a thorough check-up and found her to be perfectly healthy and unhurt apart from a cut on her paw, which he dressed and bandaged. She sat as still as a statue while he wrapped her paw with bright pink cohesive bandage.

There was an address and phone number on her tag. He knew the street. It was a quiet place with small family houses as far as he remembered. He hoped the owners took as good care of their daughter as they did their dog. She was in great shape.

The hospital would have let them know their dog was safe. Perhaps it would be Regan who gave them the good news. He still couldn't believe how amazing it had been to see her again or how much she'd changed. He supposed he'd changed too. Six years was a long time.

'I'm kidding myself, Bonnie,' he said. 'I came back here knowing full well I'd probably bump into Regan at some point. In fact I pretty much banked on it. How dumb is that? As if Regan would want to see me! Anyway, she'll have a life of her own now. She won't want me hanging around.'

Bonnie's ears lifted.

'Oh, I said something you liked? How about Georgie?'

Bonnie tried to jump down from the table. There was a name she recognised. He lifted her to the floor and she waved her bandaged foot wildly for a moment before heading straight for the door and scrabbling impatiently at it. People who said dogs didn't understand what you were talking about were out of their minds. This one understood every word.

'You know your way out, huh?' he grinned. 'Been here before have you, girl?' He couldn't check for her records on the computer because he didn't know the surname of her owners, but she was clearly one of Dennis's patients. 'You can't go yet. I doubt there'll be anyone at home. They should be at the hospital with Georgie right now.' And he wasn't about to leave her alone after all she'd been through. 'You'd better come upstairs with me and have something to eat. I hope you get on with other dogs.'

Even if she didn't, his own dogs were a friendly bunch and the cats would just roll their eyes and groan at the sight of another animal before taking themselves off to hide somewhere. And of course, if he took her to his home, he'd have to go to the hospital to let Regan know where she was, just so she could let the family know if they wanted to pick her up before morning surgery, which was in about . . . He glanced at his watch. Two hours!

'Sorry, Regan,' he said. 'Much as I want to see you again, it'll have to be a phone call.'

Bonnie barked, turned around in a circle, then sat down and looked up at him expectantly. She looked as if she was laughing.

'Funny dog,' he laughed, shaking his head. He rang the hospital, but Regan had gone home. Disappointed, he left a message for Georgie's mother confirming that Bonnie was fine and ready to be collected anytime.

Regan slid beneath the cool duvet and closed her eyes. It was no use. She would never sleep. Every time she closed her eyes she saw either Georgie with her little bloody face looking terrified as she peeked from a head brace, or Bram looking . . . well, looking so damn gorgeous, just like he always did — just like he always had.

She tossed and turned, punched her pillow into shape, then threw it on the floor. Her legs wouldn't be still and her thoughts were so loud and confused, like an incessant babble inside her head. She swung between feeling sick with fear at what could have happened and feeling sick with anticipation at what might yet happen. She was going to have to tell Bram about Georgie. She should have done it straight away and she knew the longer she left it, the harder it would be. The other thing keeping her awake was thoughts of Bonnie. She should have picked her up.

She should have told Bram then that Bonnie was her dog and Georgie their daughter. It was another missed opportunity.

'Oh, Bonnie,' she whispered, touching the bed beside her where Bonnie slept during the day when Regan was on night shifts and Georgie was at school. At night she slept on Georgie's bed, but she always liked to be close to one of them. It was just typical of her to have tried to get to Georgie, not realising she'd already been rescued. Of course she'd have been frightened off by all the rescue vehicles as well as the storm and the lights. Regan imagined her creeping back when she was sure everyone had gone.

At least she knew she'd be in safe hands with Bram. He was completely soppy when it came to animals.

* * *

When Bram emerged from his surgery, the grey-haired woman sitting in his waiting room got straight to her feet. 'I'm here for Bonnie,' she blurted.

'I know,' he said. 'She's asleep in the staffroom.' He hadn't wanted to put her in a cage when he brought her back downstairs from his flat. He didn't really know why, except she'd curled up on the small sofa and had looked so peaceful and settled, he hadn't the heart to disturb her when he had to start seeing patients. 'Sue, would you fetch Bonnie, please?' he said, then he turned back to the woman. 'She's in good shape, considering. She was cold and wet when we found her and she has a cut on her paw which was pretty clean and should heal nicely with proper care. I've put a dressing on, but I want to see her tomorrow to check it out.'

'Thank you,' the woman said as she opened her bag and pulled out her purse. 'How much is it?'

'Sorry?' Bram frowned.

'Your bill, for the dressing and everything.'

'There is no charge,' he said crisply. This had to be Georgie's grandmother. She was too old, surely, to be her mother. Perhaps there was no mother. He had to stop judging people he knew nothing about, and this poor woman looked as if she'd had hardly any sleep.

He smiled. 'How's Georgie, Mrs . . .?'

'Shires,' she said. 'Lally Shires. Everyone calls me Lally. But you must have incurred expenses, and she was quite adamant that I should pay the bill.'

'She?' Bram's eyebrows rose.

'Bonnie's owner,' Lally said and she looked the other way, unable to meet his eyes. Now what was all that about? It was almost as if she was hiding something. 'I look after Georgie and Bonnie while she's at work.'

'I see.' Bram felt his lips tighten and had to make a conscious effort to untighten them. Perhaps it was him. Regan always used to say he was like a bull at a gate sometimes, scaring people with what she called his self-righteous pomposity. She always made it sound like a joke, but maybe there was some truth in it. He softened his features into a smile and Lally seemed to relax.

'She's in bed now, catching up on her sleep, poor love,' Lally went on.

''Poor love?'' he repeated incredulously. Oh there he went again, judging and deciding what was going on without having the full facts. He packed away his indignation, put the lid down firmly on top of it and smiled again.

The door from the back opened and Bonnie bounded through, ecstatic to see a familiar face. She bounced up and down, barking happily, and Lally made a huge fuss of her. She was near to tears. 'She looks great,' she said. 'Did you bath her?'

'I gave her a bit of a rinse,' he said. 'She'd got seaweed and all sorts stuck in her fur.'

'She loves the water if she's swimming in it, but not so keen on baths, are you, girl?'

Sue handed the lead to Lally and she thanked Bram again before hurrying towards the door.

'Mrs Shires . . . '

'Lally.'

'Lally.' He smiled. 'When Georgie is better, bring her down to the RNLI station. We'll show her around.'

'Oh, she'd love that,' Lally said. 'She's always been a bit of a tomboy, you know — loves her fire engines and trucks and so on. Actually she's a bit of a daredevil. It's a worry, but hopefully this will have dampened her enthusiasm for adventure a little.'

'Sometimes it is better to use that sense of adventure rather than try to suppress it,' Bram said. 'Her parents should look into some sort of after-school club she can join.'

'Parent,' Lally said, and again her eyes slid away as if she couldn't look him in the eye. 'There's just her mum. Thank you again, Mr Fletcher.'

'Bram,' he said.

'And you want to see Bonnie tomorrow?' Lally confirmed.

'That's right.'

'Ten o'clock,' Sue put in. 'I've made an appointment.' She handed a card to Lally. 'If it's not convenient, let us know. Oh, and is Bonnie one of our patients? I've only worked here for a month and I don't recognise her.'

'Yes,' Lally said. 'She . . . '

The door flew open and a man rushed in carrying a cat box. 'Please, help!' he cried. Bram ushered him straight into the surgery with an apologetic look at Lally.

Phew! Lally was wondering how she was going to tell Sue the name of Bonnie's owner without dropping Regan right in it, when Bram stuck his head out and called her.

'Need your help here, Sue,' he said. 'It's going to be an emergency C-section. See you tomorrow, Lally.'

Lally breathed a sigh of relief. All this subterfuge didn't come easily to her. Not that she'd actually lied to anyone. Yet. But until Regan had had a chance to speak to Bram, she'd have to keep up the pretence and remember not to name names. She scribbled a note for Sue: 'Just remembered, Bonnie not a patient here. Please put her account in my name. Mrs Shires.'

Oh now that was a big fat lie, and she'd put it in writing too. She bit her lip, considered screwing up the paper and chucking it in the bin, then left before she could change her mind. Whatever she did would be wrong, but dropping Regan in it was the lesser of two evils.

When she got back to Regan's, she crept upstairs and peeked around the bedroom door. Regan was sound asleep. Bonnie ran over and jumped on the bed, snuggling up beside Regan and settling down with a contented smile.

'Don't wake her up, Bonnie,' Lally whispered, but the dog's eyes were already closing. Bless them, they were both totally exhausted and would sleep for hours.

'For goodness sake,' Regan groaned, lifting her head from the pillow. 'What on earth is going on? What's all the noise about?'

Someone was hammering on the door and shouting, and Bonnie was barking like crazy. She'd been dimly aware of Bonnie jumping onto the bed at some point and had settled into a deeper sleep after that, knowing that Lally had dropped her off.

Now her mouth was dry and her head spinning. Her first confused thoughts were that Georgie had been sent home from school early, but Georgie was safe at the hospital and they'd phone if anything was wrong. She checked her phone. No missed calls.

She fought back a wave of nausea and reached for her dressing gown. The hammering and shouting continued. She'd had all of three hours' sleep.

'All right,' she called as she hurried down the stairs. 'I'm coming.' Not that her caller would be able to hear above the racket they were making as well as Bonnie's frenzied barking. Regan shut her in the living room and she continued to bark.

When she opened the door, she found herself face to face with one of her neighbours, Katie. She had a son in Georgie's class and she looked absolutely furious. 'Where is he then?' she said, pushing her way into the hall. 'Little bugger, I'll kill him when I get hold of him.'

'Sorry, who?' Regan blinked. 'What are you talking about?'

'Jay. Who else?' She looked Regan up and down. 'Were you in bed?' She sounded faintly disgusted.

'I'm working the night shift,' Regan said, stifling a yawn, though why she should have to explain herself to her angry neighbour she didn't know. Katie wasn't the easiest person to get on with. She'd moved into Coastguard Cottages a couple of years before after splitting up with her husband and she seemed to have quite a chip on her shoulder. 'Why would I know where your son is? Surely he's at school.' She wondered briefly if Jay's dad had taken him. He visited almost every weekend and seemed like

86

a nice guy — not the sort who'd take his son without the knowledge of his mother, surely. Regan had met him a few times, just to say hello, and he was very pleasant.

'Well he would be at school,' Katie snapped, 'if he wasn't off somewhere with your daughter.'

'My daughter's in hospital,' Regan said. She waited for that to sink in, then as her mind began to clear and she realised the implications of all this, she added, 'I think we should call the police.'

'No need to get them involved,' Katie said, suddenly on the defensive. 'It's just a prank. I've only just noticed he's missing. He wouldn't get up for school this morning and I left him until half an hour ago, then what happens when I go in his room? He's put stuff in his bed to make it look like he's in it, so I'd been telling a pile of clothes to shift themselves, not Jay at all. I thought he was feeling ill or something.' Her anger was rapidly vanishing, anxiety in its place.

'I'll get dressed,' Regan said. 'There's my phone. Call the police and tell them your son is missing and to start searching the cliffs.'

'The cliffs? Why? He wouldn't go up there. And what if the police find out I was letting him get a day off school when he didn't need it? I could lose him, you know! What if they decide he should live with his dad instead of me? I just couldn't face the hassle today of getting him up — that's not a crime, is it?'

'Just do it, please, Katie.'

'Why?' she said. 'What's going on? What do you think's happened to him? Why's Georgie in hospital?' She began to look really frightened now.

'Just make the call, Katie,' Regan said. 'I'll be as quick as I can.' She threw on the nearest thing to hand, her uniform. She didn't even stop to brush her hair or put on tights. Things like that had no importance when a child's life was at stake. When she came back downstairs, Katie was still standing in the hall. She hadn't made the call.

'I'll get in trouble,' she said. 'He's done that before. Pretended he was ill and refused to get up until it was too late to take him to school. I've already been in it up to my neck for his absences, and he's only six. It's not my fault. And if his dad gets wind of it, he'll take him off me. You've seen how often he's here visiting.' She rubbed her hands nervously up and down her arms and shivered.

'I'm sure he wouldn't do that,' Regan said gently.

'You don't know him. He's always coming to visit. I don't really mind because Jay loves him to bits, but maybe that's his plan. Maybe he's going to take Jay away. He said he wanted us to get back together, but I said no.'

'What made you think Jay was here?' Regan asked.

'Because he's always going on about Georgie and you know what they're like. As thick as thieves, those two.'

Regan automatically reached for her car keys, but there was no car outside.

She'd left it in the hospital car park. She grabbed her phone and ushered Katie out of the door. If only she could think straight.

'What the hell's going on?' Katie demanded. The poor woman was terrified now.

'I don't know,' Regan said. 'I need to think. You don't drive, do you? I'll call a taxi.'

She was getting her keys out, about to go back into her house, when a big four-by-four turned the corner and pulled up outside. The back of it was full of empty cages and sitting behind the wheel, checking out the houses, was Bram. Regan began to wonder if this was another nightmare. Maybe she was still asleep and none of this was real. But nightmares were an all-too-real part of her life and had been for six years. Now she seemed to be living right in the middle of one.

The car pulling up outside started Bonnie off again. Of all people it had to be him, but under the circumstances, she was mightily relieved that it was.

'What are you doing here?' Bram said as he got out of the car.

'No time to explain,' Regan replied. 'Why are you here?'

'I just came to check on Bonnie and bring some antibiotics in case that paw gets infected,' Bram explained. 'But from the barking it sounds as if no one's home. She's been left on her own already.' He said that last with a heaviness in his voice.

'No, it's . . . I'm . . . I've got to get back to the hospital. This is Katie. Could you give us a lift, Bram?'

He looked her up and down, no doubt taking in her crumpled uniform and messy hair, and a frown creased his forehead. 'Sure,' he said and he raised an eyebrow, but Regan knew he wouldn't ask questions. He could see plainly enough that something was very wrong. He cast a suspicious look at Katie, who was still wearing slippers, and told them to get in the car.

'Haven't you been to bed yet?' he asked

as he closed her door. 'You look . . . '

'Yes, I'm well aware of how I look, thank you,' she snapped. 'Bram, we have to contact emergency services. Katie's little boy is missing. She thinks he was with Georgie.'

He was getting into the car as she spoke and she saw his shoulders stiffen. 'You think he was up at the cliffs too?'

'Almost certain,' Regan replied.

'Okay. Make the call, Regan.'

It was a short drive to the hospital, especially at this time of day, when traffic was relatively light. 'Thanks, Bram,' Regan said when he pulled up in the patients' car park. 'I appreciate that.'

But he wasn't going to be easily dismissed. He got out of the car, straightening the thick black sweater he wore.

'You don't have to stay,' Regan said. 'I have my car here.'

He gave Katie another curious look. He clearly had no intention of driving off anytime soon. 'I was thinking I might pop in and see Georgie while I'm here,' he said.

'No!' The word came out as a shout that caught Katie's attention. 'That's not a good idea, Bram. It's a terrible idea actually. She'll be sleeping. You know how it is. She'll need lots of rest.'

'Yeah.' He nodded. 'You're right, and probably the last thing she needs to see is my ugly mug.'

'You're not ugly, Bram, and you know it,' Regan murmured, smiling reluctantly. 'Far from it.'

'Okay.' He grinned and sent her heart spinning out of control. 'See you around then, Regan. I hope. I'll head up and join the search.'

She nodded and watched him drive off, then gripped Katie's arm and led her into the hospital and up to the ward to see Georgie. Why did he have to add, 'I hope?' It implied that he wanted to see her again — but why would he? They were finished. He'd made that perfectly plain six years ago. All this would be so much easier if he was prickly and bad-tempered.

But she had more pressing concerns

now. She had to find out where Jay was. Georgie was awake and sitting up in bed, sticking stickers into a comic with Lally. Lally smiled when she saw them coming, but her face paled when she saw Katie. She could see at once that something was very wrong. Georgie had gone pale too. She looked terrified.

'Hi, darling,' Regan said, kissing Georgie's cheek. 'How are you feeling?'

'All right,' Georgie whispered. She hadn't taken her eyes off Katie.

'Georgie, was Jay with you last night, love?'

Lally let out a gasp. Georgie's eyes grew big and round and she shook her head.

'Come on, Georgie,' Katie said. 'I know Jay was with you. Where is he?'

Georgie shrank back against the pillows and shook her head.

'Maybe you should wait outside, Katie,' Regan said. 'I'll get her to tell me what's been going on.'

'Shall I go too?' Lally asked.

Regan nodded. 'Please.'

Lally got up and put her arm around Katie, who allowed herself to be led away, albeit reluctantly. 'Come on, love,' she said. 'Can I get you a coffee or something?'

As soon as they were on their own, Regan asked again. 'And this time,' she added, 'I want the truth. Jay might be in danger.'

'You mustn't tell her,' Georgie whispered. 'Jay ran away from home last night. There's a sort of cave in the cliff and he's going to live there. He's going to eat seaweed and catch fish and I . . . ' Her voice trembled and she bit her lip as tears splashed onto the sheets. Regan knew whatever came next was going to be bad.

'Why? Why was he running away, Georgie?'

'He said his dad would have to come and look for him and he'd only go home if his mum and dad got back together.'

Regan moaned softly. Oh, the sweet innocence of children.

'I went to be his lookout and help him carry stuff,' Georgie went on, fighting hard to control her sobs. 'We took Bonnie with us, but Jay said she might fall off the cliff so he tied her up with some rope. She was so scared, Mummy. It was noisy . . . the wind and the waves and the rain, and I think there was thunder . . . and it was so dark.' She pressed her knuckle against her mouth and shuddered.

'It's all right, love.' Regan gathered Georgie in her arms and held her close. She was trembling all over. Poor Bonnie. It would have been torture for her being tied up in the dark with all the noise of the storm. No wonder she was so scared. 'Just tell me what happened.'

Georgie drew in her breath sharply. 'Bonnie was howling and I went to get her, but when I untied the rope she pulled away and ran. I couldn't catch her.'

'Did Lally tell you Bonnie is okay?' she asked.

Georgie nodded. Well that was something. At least Georgie wasn't worrying herself silly over the dog. 'She said Bram saved her.'

'Yes, that's right. He did.'

'And she's not hurt or anything?'

'She has a sore paw, but it'll heal. What happened next, Georgie?'

'I went back to find Jay, but he'd gone. I was scared and my torch went out and I ran, too, and . . . and then . . . '

'Shh, it's all right, baby, I know the rest,' Regan soothed. 'You don't have to tell me any more now. And don't worry, Jay won't get into trouble, I promise. But he can't live in a cave — you know that, don't you?'

Georgie nodded and Regan just hoped the boy had made it to the cave and was still there.

6

It seemed as if the whole town had turned out to search for Jay. His mother was full of what she was going to do to him when she got hold of him and Regan didn't believe a word of it. Katie was just desperate and almost out of her mind with fear and worry. Regan herself was filled with trepidation. If they found him — and it was a very big if — then the chances of him being unhurt were slim.

Over twelve hours had passed since Georgie's rescue and the tide was high again, which hampered their efforts. The weather had calmed, the rain had stopped, and the *Molly Jane* was patrolling a few hundred metres from shore, but as the tide began to recede there was still no sign of the little boy.

Regan stood apart from everyone else on the beach. She felt numb with exhaustion, but knew if she went to bed right now she wouldn't be able to sleep knowing another child was out here somewhere, especially when that child was Jay.

'I'm going to head along the beach towards the cliff,' a voice said as a hand gripped her arm. 'You coming?'

'Bram!'

'None other,' he said grimly. 'I had no idea there was another kid out here last night. If I had . . . '

'Don't blame yourself,' Regan said. 'There was no way anyone could have known Jay was out here. Georgie was so determined not to betray her friend. She's a very loyal little girl.'

'Well,' he said, 'I'd certainly want her on my team. What were they playing at, do you know?'

'Jay thought if he ran away from home, he could blackmail his parents into getting back together,' Regan explained.

'Ah, kid-logic,' he said. 'And is there any chance of that happening?'

'I don't know,' Regan sighed. 'They've lived apart for a couple of years, but he's been around a lot lately.'

'A kid needs both parents,' Bram said fiercely.

'In a perfect world,' Regan muttered. 'Sometimes two parents aren't any better than one. Sometimes they're worse. There are no ideals.' She knew that from experience.

He stood, bracing himself on the rocks, staring up and down the beach. There was still enough of a breeze to ruffle his hair. Then he looked down at her and her heart flipped.

'You're hardly dressed for the beach,' he said, and Regan was aware of her lightweight jacket, the one she wore to drive or to go shopping. The chill went right through it and she felt cold in her bones. Her uniform wasn't meant for outdoors, her bare legs were frozen, and her shoes were already rubbing her heels. A little discomfort was nothing though; she didn't want to leave the search just to find something different to wear. All that mattered was finding Jay.

Before she could say anything, Bram was sliding his leather jacket from his shoulders and holding it for her.

'Oh, no, I couldn't.'

'Stop arguing and put it on,' he said. 'At least wear it till you warm up a bit. You're freezing and the last thing we need is people collapsing on us.'

'Don't worry. If I collapse I'll try not to knock anyone else over,' she said, and he laughed softly.

The jacket was warm from his body and smelled faintly of him. She nestled inside its soft lining and remembered when she'd felt the direct warmth of his body rather than his second-hand but very welcome heat.

'You okay over the rocks?'

She nodded. 'I'm pretty sure the cave Jay was planning to live in is just around here. I used to play in it when I was a kid. We all did. My parents would have had a fit if they'd known.'

'You?' Bram laughed. 'Climbing cliffs?'

She bit her lip and gave him a sheepish smile. Maybe Georgie hadn't got all her recklessness from her father's side after all. Come to think of it, she had been quite a little daredevil herself when she was little. Nothing used to frighten her. It was only when she grew up and fell in love that she truly began to know the real meaning of fear. And now she was a parent, her fear knew no bounds. She hadn't been able to live with the fear of losing Bram, but when it came to her daughter she had no choice: there was no walking away. She'd learned a lot from being a mother. If only she'd had that knowledge before she let Bram go.

'I was young once you know,' she said lightly. 'We used to make camps in there. But Bram, we always climbed up from the beach, not down from the cliff top.' She shivered, thinking of Jay trying to climb down the side of the cliff in last night's storm. He must have been driven by such desperation.

Some of the others were approaching

from the other end of the beach, and more people were up on the top or further down near the dunes searching the beach huts. Eventually they'd meet the people coming from the opposite direction, and by then the tide would be out further and they would start searching along the water's edge, following the tide out, hoping against hope there was nothing to find on the shore.

'Are you limping?' Regan asked.

'Me? No! Well, maybe a little,' he said. 'Might've twisted my ankle a bit last night, but . . .'

'But nothing! What are you doing down here climbing about over rocks?' Regan sighed. 'You don't change do you, Bram? How can you expect anyone to care about you when you don't give a damn about yourself?'

He gave her a look, the kind of look that turned her stomach to jelly. 'Who said no one cared about me?' he said, and she was taken aback. She'd assumed that he, like her, was still on his own. What a stupid thing to think. Bram was gorgeous — a wonderful man, so easy to love despite being the most annoying man she'd ever known. It was unthinkable that he wouldn't have been snapped up. And snapped up by someone with more courage than she had.

She stopped between the rocks and looked up at him, then took a step and her foot sank into the mud almost up to her knee. She shrieked with surprise and Bram leapt forward and grabbed her. He was laughing as he tried to pull her free of the sucky mud and Regan felt her shoe go and knew she'd just lost one of the most comfortable shoes she'd ever owned.

At last her foot came free of the mud, streaked with black and grey and minus the shoe. She wrenched herself away from Bram, pulled the other shoe off and hurled it at the sea with a yell of fury.

'Good work,' Bram said, still laughing, blue eyes twinkling. 'That'll show it.'

She was even shorter now and glared up at him furiously. 'Come on,' she said. 'We have a lost child to find. There is nothing to laugh about.'

Her words sobered him and he followed her across the rocks. She knew where she was headed and he had to follow.

What she wanted was to put as much distance between them as possible. His arms around her, even if he was pulling her out of a hole, had been ever so slightly unbearable. Not in an unpleasant way either, which made it more unbearable still. Maybe if it was unpleasant all of this would be easier to handle, but the strength of her feelings for him even after all this time had caught her completely off guard.

Bram watched her slip and slide over the rocks and step over stones and mud in her bare feet and he could hardly believe this was the Regan he knew and used to love. Used to, he reminded himself. Used to. Couldn't say it enough times, but he was yet to convince himself that there was any 'used to' about it. She was as sure-footed as a wading bird and knew exactly where to step and where to avoid. He followed closely in her footsteps.

All that time they'd been a couple, living together, loving each other, and he'd never seen this side of her; never seen the beach urchin she truly was. Regan had always been a little bit prim up there on her high horse. It felt strange to see her with her feet firmly planted on the ground.

In some places she stretched her arms out to her sides for balance, but the sleeves of his jacket were so long on her that her hands disappeared. In other places she hopped from rock to rock like a mountain goat. It was fascinating to watch, but Bram kept one eye on the ground around them, looking for evidence he hoped not to see.

'My God!' She stopped dead ahead of him, staring at something caught between the rocks.

'What is it?' He hurried to her side as she bent down and picked up a small red shoe.

'It's Georgie's,' she whispered, hugging it against her chest. The little shoe was sodden wet and full of sand. Green weed had stuck to the Velcro strap. The tide must have picked it up and spat it out again.

'I don't expect she'll want it back,' he said.

But it was strange; the sight of that little shoe had been like a kick in the stomach for him too. It was a stark symbol of what could have been — how differently this could have ended for that little girl. Strange to feel so emotional about a kid they'd both seen for the first time last night, but what a kid!

'Throw it away, Regan. It's no use now it's been in the sea. Her parents won't want it back.'

But she was hugging it against her as if her life depended on it and big fat tears were rolling down her face. He'd seen her get emotional before, usually when she was dead on her feet and often when he'd got hurt.

Yet at Tom's funeral she'd been icily

calm. Pale-faced. Cool. No tears. He blinked the memory away because every time he thought about Tom, he remembered how he'd hung on to him in the water, telling him they were going to be okay. They'd got to be. Tom had two small children. But he hadn't been okay. Even as Bram struggled to keep him afloat, it was already too late. The only thing Bram had been able to do was to spare Tom's widow of the agony of waiting for a body to wash up on the beach.

There was nothing icy or cool about Regan now. She was coming apart at the seams! Her nose had gone red and when she looked up at him, eyes huge and moist with tears, he felt a kick in his gut. She cuffed the end of her nose with the heel of her hand. He reached out for her, but she took a step backwards and he could see she was making a huge effort to compose herself.

'It's up there,' she said, pointing up the cliff. 'The cave.' She pressed the shoe into his hands. 'I'll go up and see if there's any sign of him,' she went on.

'No, you . . .'

'Oh, pipe down, Bram! You don't have to do every damn thing yourself, you know, and I've done this a lot of times. With your twisted ankle and your sore back — and don't tell me it isn't sore! I saw you wincing when you were going over the rocks — there's no way you're climbing up there.'

There was no point arguing the toss with her. He knew from experience that once Regan Tyler had made up her mind about something, there was no stopping her. And she was right: his back was sore. Worse than sore, and his ankle was giving him hell. There was no way he wanted to climb up that cliff. But he didn't want her doing it either. He hadn't come back here and found her again only to promptly lose her. He still had quite a lot of work to do as far as Regan Tyler was concerned, but he hadn't given up hope just yet.

She hurried over to the foot of the cliff and looked up, no doubt planning her route. He tapped her on the shoulder and she turned round. 'Actually, I was going to say I'd call one of the other guys to go up, Regan,' he said quietly, and he could practically see the wind falling out of her sails. 'I might be reckless, but I'm not stupid, and I don't think you are either.'

'I know what I'm doing,' she said, and before he could stop her, she was crawling up the rock like a spider. After all she'd said to him about putting his life in danger, there she was doing exactly the same thing. Okay, it wasn't a high climb, but it was a slippery one; and if she fell she probably wouldn't kill herself, but if she hit her head . . .

'Regan, wait!'

She was finding purchase on the slippery, weed-covered rocks and grasped a handful of weed to pull herself up, but it broke free. He couldn't be sure, but he could have sworn he heard her fingernails snap. He held up his arms ready to catch her, but she halted her slide and carried on up, more determined than ever. This was not the Regan Tyler he knew, or thought he knew. The Regan Tyler he knew wouldn't be climbing up rocks, and she'd definitely be more coy about showing off her underwear.

'What are you laughing at?' she called down.

'Just enjoying the view.'

'Look the other way, Fletcher.'

He stopped laughing, reminding himself why she was climbing up the cliff. You had to laugh sometimes or you'd go mad, but he had an awful feeling that there wouldn't be anything to smile about today. 'Just be careful,' he said soberly.

Regan pushed herself forward onto her stomach and slithered into the shallow cave. Amazing how the technique all came back to her despite it being many years since she'd done it. It hurt a lot more now, though, than it did when she was a kid.

There were signs of a camp, but it was an old one, probably left over from last summer, which was when the local kids tended to play down here. Some things never changed, she thought wryly. Kids were always up for a bit of adventure away from the television and computer games.

But it meant that Jay hadn't been here. She was bitterly disappointed. She'd hoped to crawl in and find him huddled up in blankets looking sorry for himself, or at least to find some of his stuff.

And now she had to get back down again. How could she have forgotten how hard that was? Getting up to the cave was the easy part. Getting down was another animal entirely. Getting down was cutting yourself on sharp barnacles and jagged stone and bruising yourself on lumps of unforgiving rock. And it was one thing to get those kind of wounds when you were ten years old and shrugged off such things, but when you were a grown woman of twenty-nine with a lot less bounce and a lot more fear, it was quite another.

And why oh why hadn't she grabbed trousers when she got dressed?

Just how did she used to do it? She looked up. There was always the choice of keeping on right to the top. At least then she wouldn't have to look down. When she did look down she saw Bram looking up at her, arms folded across his broad chest, and fought back a wave of dizziness. Ugh, it looked a long way to the bottom.

'Nothing,' she called down, trying to hide the wobble in her voice. 'No sign of him at all.' She wasn't sure if that was a good or a bad thing. Her heart hoped it was a good thing, but her head told her something else. Georgie said he'd disappeared, and Jay wasn't the sort of boy to have gone off and left Georgie behind. Not deliberately.

'Come on down then,' he said. He knew very well that coming down was harder than going up. She had no idea how to even start.

'I can't,' she admitted.

'Why not? You want to stay up there and live in a cave? Your bed would get wet every time there was a spring tide and you'd end up smelling like a fish.'

Damn him, this wasn't funny. She was tired, wrung-out, and she just wanted to be back on the beach so she could continue looking for Jay, who was probably hiding out somewhere with absolutely no idea that such a big search was taking place. At least she still hoped he was, because she was not going to listen to that voice in her head telling her they were too late.

Maybe he hadn't disappeared at all. Perhaps he was there and saw Georgie go over the cliff and panicked. He might even have made his way home and be hiding under his bed or something equally daft. She hoped so. She hoped so with all her heart.

'Want me to come up and get you?'

'No!' she said. 'Not with your back and your ankle.'

'Well I can't leave them on the beach,' he said.

'Oh, ha ha,' she said sarcastically, but still she couldn't stop a smile twitching the corners of her lips.

He looked up and grasped a handful of weed, shoving his foot into a dent in the rocks.

'Bram, don't you dare come up here. Stay where you are. I'll get down somehow, and if I can't, then . . . ' She looked upwards. 'I'll just keep going up. I've done it before.' Going up was easier than coming down.

'Now that really would be stupid,' Bram said, and he was already six feet off the beach. 'I'm not coming all the way up to you, just far enough to guide you down. Okay?'

She wanted to tell him to get lost, but she knew she needed help and there was nothing to gain by trying to do it on her own. Except maybe a few broken bones and a badly bruised ego. 'Okay,' she said reluctantly, and when he was just a few feet below her, he told her to turn around and come back down towards him.

'I'll guide your feet into place,' he said. 'Trust me.'

Trust him? But what choice did she

have? Very soon others would join them and she'd be showing off her lack of climbing skills, not to mention her knickers, to half the town.

'Okay, Regan — keep coming, keep coming . . . steady . . . That's it. There.' He reached up and guided her foot into a dip. 'Now the other one. Slowly, honey. Relax. You're doing fine.'

It went perfectly well until her foot slipped and she began to slide. Her knees scraped painfully against the rock and she landed back against Bram, pushing him away from the cliff face and sending them both into a fall. She screamed, but it was cut abruptly short. They'd only fallen a few feet and she'd landed on top of him, luckily on the sand. 'Are you all right?' she cried, struggling to get off him. 'Did I squash you?'

'No,' Bram groaned. 'It's my chest. I think you crushed my ribs. I can't breathe . . . '

'Oh, Bram!' She knelt down beside him. 'I'm so sorry. I knew I shouldn't have let you discharge yourself. You're obviously not fit, and now . . . '

He began to shake. It took a moment to realise he was laughing. He propped himself up on his elbows and grinned at her. 'I think you broke my heart, Nurse.'

'Oh! What? You!' She scrambled to her feet and kicked him in the thigh with her bare foot, which was sore as well as freezing cold. Then she wrenched off his jacket and flung it at him. She'd forgotten this side of him: the teasing; the way he could wind her up so easily. She'd completely buried the fun and laughter they used to have and had chosen to just remember the serious, determined Bram Fletcher who had scared her to death every time he went out on a shout. It had been like a dark cloud over their relationship, shadowing everything they did, always there at the back of her mind. *What if he gets called out on a shout? What if he doesn't come back?* He'd told her she had too much imagination.

'Regan . . . wait . . . '

'This is not funny,' she said. 'We're meant to be looking for Jay, not all this stupid messing about.'

He grabbed her arm and swung her back round. His face was deadly serious, his expression as dark as she'd ever seen it. 'Don't for one minute think I don't realise how serious this is,' he said, his voice gravelly. 'I want to find that kid safe and well as much as you do.'

'I know,' she whispered. She turned away from him and started to stamp across the rocks, not taking such care as before. Then she remembered Georgie's shoe and turned to sweep it up from the sand where Bram had dropped it. Her knees were raw and bleeding, her fingers likewise, and as she spun away from him again she caught sight of a little pile of rags standing proud of the outgoing tide. Just a dark heap.

'Oh, my God,' she whispered. 'Oh no . . . Jay . . . ' She ran out. There weren't so many rocks, but more tiny stones, more areas of sinky mud and more slippery clay flats, and she had to fight to keep her balance. All the time she ran, she prayed this was just what it looked like, a heap of old clothes. She was aware of feet slapping on the mud behind her and as she reached the pathetic little mound, Bram was beside her, both of them breathing hard.

'Oh no,' Bram muttered.

Jay was a scruffy little boy, smaller and skinnier than the other kids in the class. His hair was too long, always untidy, and his clothes were literally coming apart at the seams in some cases. He'd go off to school in the mornings looking neat and smart, but by the end of the day he looked as if he'd been dragged through a hedge. He had the cheekiest little grin and the most sparkly eyes.

'Oh, Jay,' she sobbed and bit on the back of her hand, tasting salt and blood. His black hair was matted with sand and blood, and God only knew how many bones he'd broken when he'd fallen to the rocks; she could only hope he wasn't conscious when it happened.

She brushed his hair back from his face. He was so cold. She couldn't let this happen. She turned him onto his back and prepared to perform CPR, but Bram reached out and stopped her. 'It's much too late, Regan. He's been dead for hours.'

She could see that — she wasn't stupid! It was just that she wanted him to be alive, wanted to breathe life back into his little body. She didn't want to have to tell his poor mother that she'd lost her child. How could anyone live through pain like that? It was unbearable.

She prayed his death had been instantaneous as she gathered the little boy up in her arms, held him against her chest and wept. He was so white. So white and so very cold.

This cheeky little boy had taken Georgie under his wing when she started school and although he was little, he was tough. He and Georgie insisted they were going to get married when they grew up and eat pizza for tea every day. They helped each other with their reading and sat next to each other at school.

'I'll get . . . ' Bram began, but he choked on the words. There was nothing he could get. Nothing that would bring this child back. And instead of trying to get anything, he sank onto the mud beside Regan and folded his arms around her and the little boy.

A shout went up in the distance. Help was coming, but it was too late. No one could do anything.

Bram wasn't weeping like Regan, but she could feel the ragged catch of his breath and the tremors shaking his whole body. His arms tightened around her and she leaned against him and sobbed.

★ ★ ★

Regan sat down in the quiet hospital corridor and buried her face in her hands. Her eyes were sore and swollen, but no matter how awful she felt, she knew it was nothing compared to how Katie was feeling. The poor woman. She'd collapsed when the news was broken to her and then she'd started to blame Georgie. 'If she hadn't encouraged him, he'd never have gone to the cliffs!' she'd screamed.

Regan didn't know if that was true or not, but one thing was certain: she was not going to let Georgie carry the burden of guilt for the rest of her life. They were just kids. What had happened was a terrible, tragic accident for which no one was to blame.

Katie had even lashed out, punching Regan in the chest, but her punch had no power and she'd collapsed into Regan's arms, sobbing before Lally drew her gently away and took her home.

And then she had to tell Georgie. It was the most painful, most difficult thing she'd ever had to do and she couldn't help but feel, despite not wanting to blame anyone, that none of this would have happened if she hadn't split up with Bram when she did. Perhaps having a father around would have curbed Georgie's wild streak. No, no that was silly. If Jay hadn't taken Georgie with him, it would have been someone else. And even if Bram was around, it wouldn't necessarily have stopped Georgie running off like that to help a friend.

But what was even sillier was the realisation that her whole break-up with Bram had been so stupid, so futile. Of course the world needed men like him who were willing to put their lives on the line to save others. Thanks to her and her stubbornness, her daughter was growing up without a father — a father who would have adored her given half a chance.

They wanted to keep Georgie at the hospital for another night and she was quite happy about that. She'd made friends with a little girl in the next bed and having spent time in the hospital creche as a toddler, she was very familiar with the place.

Regan knew she should go home, but once she'd sat down, the weariness had overwhelmed her. Lally had already left, taking Katie home and promising to take Bonnie for the night just in case Regan got any silly ideas about staying over at the hospital. She could use one of the on-call rooms, she supposed. If she could gather up the energy to actually move.

7

Bram saw his last patient out of the door, then locked up. Everyone had been so good about their delayed appointments. Not a single person had complained. Most people had heard about the little boy and word had quickly got round that Bram had been involved in the rescue.

He still felt numb with shock. There was nothing as bad as losing a child, and every time he closed his eyes he saw Regan with Jay in her arms. But they'd saved Georgie. He had to hold on to that. It was, after all, the successes that kept you going, knowing that you could and would make a difference in the majority of rescues.

He took his dogs for a quick walk, but in the opposite direction to the cliffs, down along where the sand dunes rolled towards the marshes. The dogs bounded along the beach, sending up clouds of geese and gulls. The wind was fresh, the scent of the sea sharp. He couldn't be sorry he came back. Nowhere he'd ever been had felt as right as this place.

Would it feel as right if Regan wasn't here? That was another matter. And the signals she was putting out were confusing. Her body was giving him a different message to her lips. Her eyes were saying, 'Welcome back, I'm glad to see you,' but her manner said, 'Keep your distance.' But it was only natural. She was bound to be wary after the way he'd left town.

Back at the surgery, he rubbed all the dogs down with towels before heading to the hospital. Josie was on duty again and she smiled when she saw him. 'Hello again, stranger,' she said. 'How are you feeling now? Regretting discharging yourself?'

'Not for a minute. I haven't come back for treatment,' he said quickly. He'd had enough of hospitals and wanted to spend as little time in one as possible. 'I know Regan's taken some time off, but I wondered if you could give me her address or phone number?'

'Oh that's nice,' Josie said. 'After all these years, all you want is Regan's phone number. Way to make a girl feel wanted!'

He grinned. 'Sorry, Josie,' he said, reaching out and giving her a friendly hug. 'How are you?'

'I'm fine, thank you. But you know I can't give you Regan's number,' she said. 'I really wish I could, but it's against regulations and besides, she'd kill me, and I'm too pretty to die.'

'She hates me that much?'

Josie smiled and shook her head. 'Of course she doesn't hate you, but it's complicated,' she said. 'You two really need to talk.'

'I'm not sure if we have anything to talk about,' he said, and was surprised at the look on Josie's face. It was almost as if she knew something he didn't. Perhaps Regan was in a relationship.

But he wouldn't press her. Her loyalties would lie with Regan, and rightly so. It wasn't fair to put her in a difficult position.

'It was worth a try.' He grinned again. 'So I guess there's no chance of you leaving Regan's number on the pad there and turning the other way while I write it down like they do in the movies?'

'No chance at all,' Josie said. 'Sorry, Bram. I wish I could.'

'It was worth a try. Georgie still here?'

'Yes, but . . . '

'It's okay,' he said. 'I know where she is and I promise I won't tread on any toes. I'll be nice as pie to her family.'

'Wait, Bram. You don't understand,' Josie said.

'What don't I understand, Josie?'

She clamped her lips together. 'What I mean is, her family will probably be with her, and you know what hospitals are like about too many visitors.'

'Don't let it worry you,' he said. 'I'm

just going to drop a gift off, then I'll leave.' He turned to go and Josie ran round in front of him.

'You don't want to do that,' she said. 'I mean, you can't go around taking presents to everyone you rescue. You'd soon be broke.'

He shook his head. 'I always get a little something when it's a kid,' he said. 'Always have. It's nice for me to see them in one piece again, especially if they were hurt like Georgie.'

'Oh, yes,' she said with a sigh. 'I see your reasoning, but . . . '

'Sorry, Josie; I think you're needed.' He saw the young doctor — Karen, wasn't it? Now instead of keeping Josie talking, he tried to hurry away.

'Not so fast, you,' Karen called out. 'How are you?' She stood on her toes and flashed her penlight in his eyes.

'What did you do that for?'

'To see if there was anything in there,' Karen said. 'I hear you were on the beach again helping look for the little boy.'

'Yes; what of it?'

'You should be resting,' she said. 'You certainly shouldn't be hanging around here, unless you've come back for treatment?'

'I was looking for Regan,' he said.

'Well, you won't find her here, as I expect Josie has told you. I suggest you go home.'

'Thanks for the suggestion,' he said. 'But I'll decide myself where I go.'

'Impossible man.' Karen sniffed. 'I don't know what they all see in you.'

He stared after her as she flounced off. What was it with women always bossing him about? Josie flashed him a look, then hurried off behind Karen. And what did she mean, she didn't know what they all saw in him? No one saw anything in him!

Unless Regan . . . He smiled, then quickly banished it. No, Regan wasn't the sort to reveal her feelings to anyone. She'd always been a very private person. So was he. That was one of the many reasons they got along so well.

Correction — used to get along so well.

He stopped at the little hospital gift shop and bought a balloon and a small toy dog before taking the lift up to the ward. Normally he avoided lifts like the plague, but it seemed every bone in his body ached and the stairs were too much like hard work.

When the lift doors opened, he looked along the corridor and saw someone sitting on a chair, head in hands. He almost backed into the lift, reluctant to intrude on someone's private grief, but gradually it sunk in exactly who it was sitting there all alone, and his first instinct was to rush down there, pick her up and cradle her in his arms.

He almost pressed the button to go back down, but he'd done enough running away. It was time to start facing up to things and one of them, the only one that mattered, was Regan.

Common sense stepped in. If he did rush down there and start hugging her, she was likely to give him a kick! But since when did common sense have anything to do with anything? She needed a hug. She was alone. He was here. It was a no-brainer.

She looked so desolate, so small and alone, that he found himself striding manfully towards her — well as manful as he could be with a limp! He stopped in front of her and she stared at his shoes, then her gaze moved slowly up to his face and she let out a gasp. 'What are you doing here?'

She looked dreadful. Her eyes were dark hollows and her skin was pale, and yet he thought he'd never seen her look so beautiful. But that wary look was there too. The one that told him to keep his distance. Maybe gathering her up for a cuddle wasn't such a great idea after all.

'I might ask you the same,' he said, sitting down beside her, still clutching the balloon and the toy. 'I just popped in to see Georgie.'

'Oh, did you?' She seemed wary and suspicious. 'Why?'

'Because I feel sorry for the kid,' he said. 'She's been through a lot and now she's lost her best mate. Apart from that, I've seen nothing of her parents. I mean if it was you or me, wild horses wouldn't drag us away from her bedside, am I right?' She looked down at her hands, but he was sure he was right and that she would agree with him, even if she'd never admit it.

'You have no idea what you'd do in this position,' she said softly. 'You can't judge other people when you can't possibly know what their situation is.'

'I wasn't. I didn't mean . . . ' He sighed, exasperated. If he wanted to convince her that he'd changed, he wasn't doing a very good job of it. 'I really didn't mean to sound so judgemental. I just wanted to see her and give her these.'

Regan looked at the balloon and the toy and her face softened into a smile. 'She'll love those.'

'So what's your excuse for being here when you should be at home catching up on your sleep, Regan?'

'I just wanted to see Georgie too,' she replied. 'I'm supposed to be going straight home, but I came over so tired, I had to sit down. I may stay here overnight. I've nothing to go home for.'

She didn't sound self-pitying. It was just as if she was stating a fact. He was glad she had no one to go home to, but at the same time he ached for her. Someone like Regan, with so much love to give, should have someone to go home to. Oh, but she didn't say that, did she? Having nothing to go home to and nothing to go home for were two different things.

'Is it really so bad that you want to sleep here?' he said. 'You used to hate sleeping over at the old hospital, do you remember? You reckoned it was haunted.'

She shivered and laughed self-consciously. 'It was!' she said. 'You'd hear noises at night, doors opening and closing, and sometimes I woke up with the feeling someone else was in the room.'

'Yes, I remember,' he said. 'You reckoned it made your hair stand on end.'

'It did!' She laughed.

'Your hair used to be so short that it used to practically stand on end anyway.'

'Thanks!'

'I like it like this.' He lifted a handful of her untidy, tangled hair and ran it through his fingers.

'Well it doesn't stand on end any more,' she said. 'There are no ghosts here.'

'Hospitals are noisy places, even at night,' he said, but he'd loved that side of her, the part that could be scared by a strange noise. Watching a spooky film with her was great. She always used to snuggle up close to him and he'd put his arm around her and pull her close. She said she felt safe in his arms. That had been such a good feeling — the best, knowing that he could make someone as self-reliant and tough as Regan feel safe.

'Bram?'

'Sorry, what?'

'You were miles away,' she said and he saw it there, the warmth in her eyes that was so inviting. Like a log fire on a cold day, drawing him in. 'I said would you like me to take the toy and balloon in to Georgie for you?'

'No,' he said. 'But I would like you to wait here. Will you do that?'

She nodded. If she tried to stand up, she'd probably fall over. That was how she looked.

'Is anyone with her? Parents?'

'No.'

The tut of disapproval was out before he could stop it and instantly that guarded look was back on her face. He cleared his throat. 'I expect it's been a very long day for them,' he said. 'It can't have been easy. And then to find out what had happened to Jay must have brought home even harder what could have happened. Probably best they've gone home. They'll want to get the kids settled for the night on the ward anyway.' He started for the door, then turned back. 'But don't they let parents stay over?'

'Sometimes,' she said.

He slipped into the ward and explained to the nurse at the desk who he was, and she said he could see Georgie for a couple of minutes. 'You must be Bram,' she said. 'Josie rang ahead and said you were on your way up.'

His heart leapt as soon as she saw her. She was out of bed and sitting on the bed of the child next to her. She wore the cutest shortie pyjamas, and her long dark hair was in two plaits. She kept flicking at the plaits, knocking them over her shoulder.

'Georgie,' he said as he approached the bed, and her name almost stuck in his throat. She really was a lovely kid. 'I don't know if you remember . . . '

'You're Bram,' she said. 'You saved me. Mummy said you were a hero!'

'Oh,' he said, pleased. A hero? He'd felt more like Mr Bean, falling over the cliff after the rescue had taken place. He handed her the balloon and the toy.

'Oh, wow, thank you,' she said,

cuddling the toy dog up tight with her good arm. 'I'll call him Lucky because I was lucky, wasn't I?' Her smile dimmed a little, then she shook away any bad thoughts she might have had and the smile returned, brighter than ever. She reminded him of a certain other young lady. Regan had always been good at doing that, blocking out the bad stuff. But it came to the point where she couldn't block it out any more and all the fear she'd been hiding bubbled to the surface and overwhelmed her. And what had he done? Instead of holding her close and chasing her fears away, he'd turned his back on her, swamped by fears of his own.

'I just came to say hello,' he said. Without all the blood, he could see just how pretty she was, with her big beautiful blue eyes and her dark hair. A pretty little girl who would grow into a stunning woman. A real heartbreaker.

'Thank you,' she said. 'You just missed my mum. She only left a little while ago. She was going to stay and sleep in the recliner chair, but Sister Judith said she'd got to go home and get some proper rest and I didn't mind.'

'That was very brave of you. I expect you'll be going home soon.'

'I'm not brave,' Georgie said, and her eyes welled with tears. The other little girl reached out and rubbed her arm, and Georgie mustered a smile and looked at Bram. 'I like it here.'

'You've been in hospital before?'

'Lots of times,' Georgie said. 'I think I'm going home tomorrow.'

'That's good. Don't forget, when you're better you're to come down to the lifeboat station and you can have a look around, okay?'

'Can I go on the boat?'

'I'm sure you can,' he laughed.

Her smile lit up her face, but suddenly it went and she shivered. Poor little kid. She was walking a tightrope, trying desperately not to fall into a well of grief. 'You all right, Georgie?' She nodded. Her eyes had gone huge and her lip trembled.

'Her best friend died,' the other little girl said. 'She keeps crying.'

'Okay,' the nurse who had been keeping an eye on them said as she came over. 'Visiting is over. We need to get these children settled for the night. Thanks for coming in. Oh, Georgie, are you crying again? Come here, sweetie.' She picked her up and carried her back to her own bed. Bram said goodbye and slipped away. Regan was watching the door when he came out.

'How was she?'

'Upset. She's right on the edge, poor little kid.'

'Was she crying again?'

'Yeah. The nurse was giving her a cuddle. She'll be exhausted on top of everything else.'

Regan got up and, almost trance-like, headed for the door back into the ward.

'Where are you going?' he said. 'The nurse said she's about to settle them down for the night.'

Still Regan looked in before moving away, then the door opened and the nurse came out. She glanced at Bram, then grabbed Regan's arm and steered her away. Regan rubbed her eyes and nodded, then the nurse hugged her and returned to the ward.

What was all that about? He had the oddest feeling . . . but no. His feelings had never been very reliable, especially when it came to Regan. 'Come on,' he said. 'I'll give you a lift home.'

'That won't be necessary,' she said, rather too quickly.

'Why not? What are you afraid of, Regan?'

'I'm not afraid.'

'Then stop being so stubborn and accept a lift. You need a decent night's sleep in your own bed. I have my car; what's to stop you? You don't hate me that much, do you?'

'You know I don't. Stop fishing for compliments.'

'I'm not looking for compliments and I don't want you to say you love me or anything daft like that. I just want to give you a lift home.'

Regan's mouth felt dry. She'd cried so much today that it felt as if every last bit of moisture had been squeezed from her body. And now here was Bram, with his big strong body into which she would love to nestle, offering her a lift home. But she couldn't accept. He'd find out where she lived. It had been a close thing earlier on and she knew he'd have to find out eventually, but not yet and certainly not tonight. She would tell him the truth — she had to — but it had to be when they were both wide awake and not feeling fragile and emotional.

'I can't go home,' she said. 'I . . . it's . . . ' *Think, think*, she told herself. *Come up with something he's going to believe.* He was watching her, waiting. She pushed her hair away from her face, aware she looked a complete mess.

'Complicated?' he said. 'Yeah, I get it.' He grabbed her wrist and gently pushed back her sleeve, exposing one of her many grazes. 'You haven't had your cuts seen to,' he said. 'Why not, Regan? After the way you lectured me about not taking care of myself.' He got to his feet and held out his hand. 'Come on,' he said. 'I'll take you down to A&E. Josie's on duty. She'll patch you up.'

'Josie? Have you seen her?'

'Yeah.' He grinned. 'I asked her for your address, but she refused to give it to me.'

She smiled. Good old Josie. Then her smile wobbled. 'Did she say anything?'

'Like what?'

Of course she hadn't. If she had, Bram wouldn't be standing there as calm as you like offering to give her a lift home. He'd be pacing up and down, demanding to know why she hadn't told him he was a father.

'It doesn't matter,' she said. 'But I don't want to go to A&E. There's no need. It's just a few scratches.'

'They need cleaning,' he said. 'All right, if you won't go home and you won't let anyone here take care of you, come home with me.'

She laughed. 'What?'

'You heard. I'm living in the flat over the surgery. You can come back, meet my dogs, and I'll practise my first-aid skills on you.'

'First-aid skills,' she laughed. That was something of an understatement. And he certainly didn't need practice with all his experience and qualifications.

'Is that a yes?'

She nodded. If she agreed to go back to his place, she could walk home from there. She would insist upon it, and he would remain in the dark about where she lived. It was all downhill from the surgery to Coastguard Cottages. She could do it in her sleep — and probably would.

He helped her to her feet, took her hand and slipped it thought his arm. 'Lean on me,' he said. 'It's what I'm here for.'

'Don't read anything into this, Bram,' she warned him. 'To be honest I'm too tired to argue the toss and it's easier to go along with you than not.'

'Pity you didn't feel that way six years ago,' he said, but he was smiling. Then he shook his head. 'I'm sorry, Regan. That came out wrong. What happened wasn't your fault.'

'Wasn't it? Anyway,' she said as they went down in the lift, 'you had a lucky escape. If we hadn't split up when we did, we'd be an old married couple by now.'

'And the problem with that is?'

She didn't have an answer. 'So where have you been for six years?'

'Here and there,' he said. 'Locum work mainly. To be honest, I didn't plan to come back, but when Dennis told me he was selling up, it was too good an opportunity to miss. The time I was here was the happiest of my life. I guess I wanted to try and recapture some of that feeling.'

'And have you?'

He stopped and looked down at her. 'Not yet, but I'm working on it. So what about you? Have you been here all the time?'

'Yup.'

'Not been tempted to marry some handsome doctor?'

'Nope.' She almost said vets were more to her liking, but if that didn't sound like an invitation, she didn't know what did, so she smiled instead.

When they got to the car, he held the door open for her and offered to fasten her seatbelt. 'I'm not helpless,' she said, cursing herself for being so sharp. He was only trying to help. This was Bram all over: the good side of him — thoughtful, considerate, kind. She had been such a fool to send him away. Not only had she denied herself the love of her life — for no man would ever, *could* ever fill the gap Bram left behind — but she'd denied her daughter the love of a wonderful father and the possibility of brothers and sisters.

8

An assortment of dogs greeted them when they arrived at the big apartment over the surgery. Regan was overwhelmed. She loved dogs and would have a houseful herself if she could. But Bram always used to say he'd wait until he had a proper home and a family before he had any pets. So what had changed?

'Where did they all come from?' she asked as she struggled to make sure each and every one got a stroke. 'They're all lovely.'

'Lovely, yes,' he said thoughtfully. 'They were all on death row at one time or another for various reasons.'

She spotted the cats, who were watching the dogs making fools of themselves, and went to tickle their ears. 'This doesn't surprise me, Bram. You always said you'd like a house full of dogs, cats and kids.' Oops, she hadn't meant to mention kids. It was tactless in the extreme, considering what she had to tell him. 'But I thought you were going to wait? And where's the border collie you always said you'd have once you settled down?'

He laughed. 'I haven't got round to that yet. I've had Pixie and Barney longest. They're ex-racing greyhounds. Then I got George, the little staffy. Fern is a staffy cross, and that little spaniel cross is called Regan.' The spaniel had chocolate curls and large brown eyes.

'You're kidding! You called your dog after me?' Regan said. She didn't know whether to laugh or cry.

'Well look at her! Same colour hair; same big, sad eyes. Besides, she didn't have a name when I got her. She was a breeding bitch from a puppy farm who'd outlived her usefulness and she was half-dead when I took her in. She's a plucky little thing though. A real fighter. I call her Rags for short.'

As soon as Regan sat down, Rags

jumped onto her lap and rested her
head on Regan's chest, gazing up at
her. Poor little thing must have been so
completely starved of affection, she was
making up for it now.

'I hate puppy farms,' Regan said
vehemently.

'So do I,' Bram said. 'The one where
Rags was kept prisoner — because it is
like being in prison, probably worse
— was shut down. We managed to find
homes for all the dogs.'

'That's so lovely — that you found
them homes, I mean.'

'I was living in a camper van,' Bram
went on. 'You might have seen it parked
out the back. It was another reason for
taking over this place. We were running
out of room.'

Regan laughed. 'I should think you
were.'

'I'm going to run you a bath and
leave you to soak while I get us something to eat,' he said.

'There's no need . . . '

'Stop turning down help when it's

offered. This is how it's going to be, Regan. You're going to have a bath and get all those cuts and grazes clean. I am going to dress them and then we are going to sit down and eat a meal together. After that I'll take you home . . . if you still want to go.'

She opened her mouth to protest, but thought better of it. A soak in the bath would be wonderful and very welcome. But of course she would still want to go. She could fight with him about walking home later on. She smelled of the beach, and while that smell was there to remind her, her thoughts constantly returned to little Jay.

'Stop torturing yourself,' Bram said, jerking her out of her thoughts. 'I can see it on your face. I know you're not going to forget about what happened, but going over and over it won't change anything.'

The dogs, as all dogs do, sensed that she was upset and had piled up around her on the sofa and on her feet. She was absent-mindedly stroking them. One of the cats had appeared on the back of the sofa behind her and was gently patting her head with a soft little paw. Trust Bram to have such kind animals!

'I'll get that bath going and leave you to your love-in,' Bram said with a grin. He left her and went across to the bathroom, pulling fresh towels from the airing cupboard and searching for something to put in the bath, something not too masculine. He found a herby muscle soak and poured it under the taps. He recalled how she used to relax in the bath with a glass of wine and scented candles. He hadn't got any fancy candles, but he did have a few bottles of decent wine.

'Regan Tyler is here, in my flat,' he said out loud and with a degree of incredulity. That was something he wouldn't have thought possible. Of course, he'd hoped when he came back that he would see her. The circumstances that had brought them together were unbearably tragic, but tragedy should bring people together, not drive them apart. He'd let it drive a wedge between them before, but it wasn't going to happen this time.

When the bath was ready, and a glass of wine poured and waiting for her, he returned to the living room and found her asleep. She looked so beautiful. He stroked her cheek gently with his finger. What he wouldn't do to have her back. She stirred when he touched her and a small smile crossed her face.

'Come on, you lot,' he said. 'Give the lady some space.' He shifted the dogs, then gently shook Regan's shoulder. She winced as she woke with a start. 'Sore shoulder?'

'Sore everything,' she said sleepily, and she stretched like a happy cat.

'Bath's ready.'

'That was quick.' She blinked as she looked around. 'Did I fall asleep?'

'You did.'

'Sorry.'

'Don't apologise. Glass of wine with your bath?'

'That would be lovely, but probably

incredibly silly on an empty stomach.' It was almost like old times, except this time he wouldn't join her in the bath or massage her aching shoulders.

'I'm afraid I don't have any candles, but the light in the bathroom is quite dim.'

'Philistine,' she laughed. He always used to tease her about her candles. He'd come home to find she'd cooked a romantic dinner and the minute he saw candles on the table he'd say, 'Oh, power cut?' It always made her laugh, and then he'd pull her into his arms and tell her how wonderful she was . . .

'Do you need any help?'

She gave him a look, half-amused, half-exasperated. 'It's a bath, Bram,' she said. 'I think I can just about manage.'

'If you need help, just shout. If you feel dizzy or anything I can give you a hand, and I promise I'll keep my eyes shut. I'll go and make a start on dinner.'

'Spag bol?' she asked.

'How did you guess?'

She laughed again. It was his signature dish and he always used a jar of sauce. It was the one thing he could make without it all going horribly wrong.

She looked round the bathroom and saw a glass of wine standing on the side. 'Really, I shouldn't,' she said, but she took a sip. 'Oh, I needed that.'

Bram had the meal well underway when he heard Rags whining out in the hall. She was outside the bathroom door. 'Come on, Rags,' he said. 'Leave her alone. She's taking a bath.' But the dog was insistent and kept clawing at the bottom of the door. In fact she was getting very agitated, almost as if she wanted to dig her way under the door. 'What's up, girl? Are you missing your new best friend?'

Rags looked up at him and backed up from the door, then went forward and began to paw it again. 'Okay,' he said, ruffling her ears. 'I'll knock. Stop worrying.' He rapped his knuckles on the door and waited for Regan to reply.

'Regan, you all right in there, honey?'

No answer. He knocked louder. There was no lock on the door, but he hesitated. He could hardly go bursting in on her. She'd kill him — or throw something at him! She wouldn't be pleased, he knew that.

'Regan,' he shouted, and Rags began to bark. The other dogs came to see what all the fuss was about, but still there was no answer from the bathroom. 'I'm coming in,' he called, pushing the door open and covering his eyes with his hand while he waited for her outraged scream. But no sound came and as he took his hand down, he realised she'd fallen asleep again, head back, hair trailing. Her modesty was intact, as she was hidden by bubbles, and the wine glass was on its side on the floor, some of the contents spilled.

'Regan.' He shook her shoulder. She felt cold. He couldn't leave her there. 'Oh, hell.' He shook her shoulder harder. 'Wake up, Regan!' he said loudly, and she jerked awake. 'There's a warm towel there. You're not going to want your dinner are you, love?' he said.

'I can't stay awake,' she said. 'Sorry, Bram.'

'It's okay. You can have my bed. I'll take the sofa. Give me a shout when you're decent and I'll come and sort out your cuts. I'll put some pyjamas out for you.'

By the time he'd fetched his first-aid box, she was on top of the bed, asleep and looking tiny in his T-shirt and shorts pyjamas. He gently dabbed antiseptic cream on her grazes and put plasters over two deeper cuts. There was nothing that needed stitches, thank goodness, but she was going to be sore in the morning. She even had blisters on her feet. One of them had burst. She must have been in a lot of pain with all this, but she hadn't complained once.

He was gently dabbing fresh blood away from her leg when he felt her eyes on him. His breath caught when he looked up and saw her watching him, her eyes soft and sleepy. 'Bram?' she murmured.

'Sh, it's okay,' he said, pulling the covers over her. 'I'm not looking, I promise. Get some sleep.' He leaned over and kissed her forehead. He was almost tempted by her parted lips, but he fought with himself and won.

He didn't trust himself at all where Regan was concerned. None of his old feelings for her had diminished. If anything, they were stronger than ever. But this time he wasn't going to leave. This time he'd see it through and if she insisted on it, he'd give up the RNLI and live the quiet life of a small-town vet. They were both older and wiser now, and if she'd missed him half as much as he'd missed her, then there had to be a chance for them.

'Go back to sleep,' he murmured, and his resolve crumbled when she reached up and put her arms round his neck, pulling him close. 'Regan, no,' he whispered. He wasn't sure he could fight her as well as himself. 'You don't know what you're doing.' He felt her breath warm against his neck and it took every ounce of willpower he possessed to push her back against the pillows. Her eyes were closed.

'Goodnight, sweetheart,' he murmured. 'Sleep tight.' And as he walked away and closed the door, he didn't know whether to kick himself or pat himself on the back.

Regan was running across the sand and all she could hear was the pounding of her feet and her own ragged breaths. 'Georgie!' she cried. 'Georgie!'

There was a bundle of clothes at the water's edge and she could see one little foot poking out and the little foot wore a red shoe. Georgie had begged for the red shoes and in the end, Regan had given in. *She can wear red shoes every day forever, just make her safe*, she sobbed.

Georgie's long dark hair was tangled with seaweed and Regan brushed it off her face. Her little girl stared up at her with Bram's eyes, but they were lifeless.

She was dead. 'Georgie! No!' she screamed. 'No!'

And then Bram was there, pulling her away, wrapping his arms around her and holding her close. She struggled to get away from him. She had to save her daughter.

'Regan, it's okay,' he said. 'It's all right.'

'Georgie,' she sobbed, reaching out, but her hands found only fur and a wet nose; and when she opened her eyes she realised she was in bed and lying next to her was Bram's dog, Rags, tail flicking, eyes filled with concern.

She sat up, breathing hard. Her body was crushed against Bram's and when she realised, she tried to push him away, but there was no strength in her hands. She was filled with righteous indignation, but the terror of her nightmare overwhelmed her and she relaxed in his arms and gave way to the tears again.

'You had a bad dream, Regan,' he soothed, holding her close, stroking her hair. He had such gentle hands. She buried her face in his shoulder and he smelled so good, and his skin against hers felt wonderful. But how could anything feel wonderful when she felt so wretched? It was a dream, but it had felt so real. She shuddered violently. She really should put a stop to this right now, but it felt so good to be held; to have someone to lean on. She couldn't remember the last time anyone had held her like this . . .

Oh, yes she could. It had been Bram, the night before he went out and nearly got killed. The feelings she'd felt that last time they were together flooded back. Then, as now, she'd felt safe in his arms. Loved. Wanted. Precious. All the things she'd never felt before in her whole life. They'd fallen asleep after planning their wedding, talking about the children they would have; the future. Then his pager had bleeped and he was leaping out of bed, bumping into things as he tried to get dressed in the dark. She'd put the light on, unaware that the future was about to be snatched away from them.

'What is it?'

'Shout,' he'd said, leaning over to kiss her. 'Go back to sleep. I'll be back in time for breakfast.'

'Be careful,' she'd told him, and she had lain awake listening to the raging storm with a terrible feeling of foreboding.

Her phone had rung just before dawn. It had been Len. 'I'm sorry, Regan,' he'd said. 'There's no easy way to say this, love. Bram's in hospital. It's bad . . . I'm heading over there now and I'll swing by and pick you up in five minutes.'

'What happened?'

'I'll fill you in when I see you.'

She'd hardly been able to dress herself, she was shaking so much. He said it was bad. How bad?

Her breathing steadied. Bram thought she'd fallen asleep and he lay down next to her, still holding her close as he pulled the duvet over her and tucked it round her so they weren't touching. He was only flesh and blood after all, and it had been a very long time . . .

He thought about the new equipment he wanted to get for the surgery; forced himself to think about work. He had to. Maybe he should think about taking on another vet. There was plenty of work for two, but did he really want more spare time on his hands? Wasn't it better to keep busy?

Regan was hardly aware of Bram lying beside her, she was so lost in her thoughts of long ago: that awful night when Len's car had pulled up outside the cottage she and Bram shared. It was raining hard and she was soaked through.

She remembered it all so vividly: running to the car, splashing through a puddle and drenching both feet.

All she could hear was Len's voice telling her it was bad. She'd got in the car. 'How is he?'

'It's a possible spinal injury,' Len said, getting straight to the point. 'Broken bones. Internal injuries. He's pretty badly smashed up, Regan. But, love, it's worse than that.'

'What can be worse?'

'Tom,' he said, and he hadn't been able to say more. She'd watched tears run down his face, shining in the lights from the dash.

'Dead?' she whispered. 'Oh, God, no!' She was silent as Len set off for the hospital, thinking of Tom's wife — his widow and his kids. There had been times like this before when Bram had got hurt. He was brave and he was reckless, but he'd always scraped through with minor injuries. Not this time.

'Is Bram going to be okay?' she whispered at last.

'No way of knowing just yet.'

'What happened, Len?'

He'd told her the story bit by bit as they drove through the night. They'd been called out to a fishing boat that had sustained serious damage. The sea had been heavy and a seventeen-year-old had been badly hurt. Bram had got the teenager stabilised, and while they were getting him into the lifeboat, the fishing boat had lurched violently. Tom was thrown into the sea, knocked unconscious, and Bram had gone in behind him. And then they'd lost them both in those raging seas and when they found them, Bram was clinging on to Tom, but he'd been battered against the side of the boat and his own injuries were just about as bad as they could get.

Her memories became hazy as once again sleep overwhelmed her. But the memories weren't going to let her go and she took them into her dreams.

They arrived at the general hospital to find that Bram had already been transferred to the spinal injuries unit at another hospital. 'I'll call my parents, Len,' Regan said shakily. 'It's not right to expect you to do all this.'

He'd waited while she made the call. Her mother hadn't been best pleased to be woken up so early in the morning. 'It's Bram,' Regan had sobbed down the phone. 'He's been hurt.'

'That's awful, darling,' her mother had replied. 'I hope he's all right.'

'No, he's not. He's been transferred to another hospital. Mum, could you or Dad drive me?'

There'd been a slightly stunned silence on the line. Regan realised she'd never asked her parents for anything before. Certainly not since she was a very small child.

'Darling, it's so early and you know neither of us likes driving in this awful weather.'

'Yes, I know but . . . '

'We would, like a shot, darling, but we've got the Andersons staying with us. What would it look like if we just disappeared? And it's not as if Bram's your husband.'

Oh, she had to get that dig in, even now when Bram's life was hanging in the balance. 'Mum, I need — '

'Look, you knew the risks when you took up with a man like Bram. If you wanted a quiet life, you should have chosen someone else. Someone like your father.' Incredibly, she heard her father chuckle in the background.

'Bram could die!' she'd yelled.

'I'm sure it won't come to that . . . '

Before she could say any more, Len had taken the phone out of her hand. 'Don't worry about your daughter,' he'd said. 'I'll take care of her. Fortunately she has many friends who will help and support her.' And then he hung up.

Sometimes in the dream her father's chuckle turned to loud, mocking laughter, and sometimes her mother said they'd be there right away. The truth was that right then, all she had was Len. 'Come on, girl,' he'd said. 'You're coming with me.'

Despite all her experience, when she walked in and saw Bram so broken up, with machines all around him and a vicious-looking cut on his face, her knees had given way and Len had caught her.

'Do you know his next of kin?' the doctor had asked.

'I think that would be me,' Regan

said shakily, remembering how he'd told her about the deaths of his grandparents within days of each other, so devoted that they couldn't live one without the other. His grandfather, he said, died of a broken heart. He was estranged from his father and she had no idea how to go about contacting him, and his mother had died when he was a child.

The doctor told her to expect the worst, but to hope for the best, and she'd sat beside his bed for days — holding his hand, talking to him, urging him to get better.

She was there again now, in her dreams and this part never changed. It was always the same. She was sitting beside his bed, holding his unresponsive hand, and then the alarm had sounded and all hell had broken loose as the room filled with doctors and nurses, and she was pulled gently out of the way.

'Bram!' she screamed, struggling to get back to him. 'Bram! Wake up! Don't you dare die on me!'

9

Bram jerked awake. It was still dark and she was screaming again, and this time it was his name she was calling out. He shook the sleep out of his head and sat up.

'I'm not going to die,' he said, shaking her gently. 'I'm here. I'm all right.' He flicked on the light and her eyes shot open. She sat up and began to hit him. 'I can't stand it,' she cried. 'You've got to stop!'

Stunned, he felt the sharp slaps of her hands before he came to his senses and managed to grasp her wrists and hold her still. 'Regan,' he said, trying to break through as he shook her gently. 'Regan, wake up! You're having another nightmare.'

She carried on struggling, but he could feel her growing weaker as wakefulness overcame sleep and she realised where she was. She looked around, seeing properly this time, her eyes full of pain and confusion. 'Bram,' she whispered. 'You're all right . . . I thought . . . It was a dream, just a dream.'

'Has this happened before? Or is it because I've just come back and because . . . because of Georgie and Jay?' He watched it all dawn on her, all the things that had happened so recently, and he saw a mask of sadness settle over her lovely face.

Voice thick with misery, she said, 'It's happened before. Not so much as it did at first, but every now and then it all comes back. Usually if I'm very tired or stressed. Anxiety dreams, I suppose.'

'I'm so sorry,' he said, cradling her in his arms again. 'I'm so very sorry, Regan. I had no idea.'

'I always wake myself up at the same part . . . It was when you had to be resuscitated. You came so close to dying, Bram, and I had to stand helplessly by and watch. I thought I'd lost you.'

Guilt washed over him in waves. How

selfish he'd been. He'd never seen things from this side before. He'd only ever seen her worried face looming over him and her demands that he must give up the RNLI. He just hadn't been able to tell her that his return to the service was in question anyway, and her demands pointless. He'd responded instead by quoting facts and figures at her. He'd been unlucky, that was all. And then came her ultimatum. It was like a lifeline and he'd grabbed it with both hands.

'Make up your mind, Bram. Me, or the RNLI?'

He hadn't wanted it to end that way, but it was too good an opportunity to miss. Let her go before she became obligated to stay. She made it easy for him. 'If I walk out that door, Regan, it's the last you'll see of me, I promise you that.' What a stupid thing it had been to say, considering he was in a wheelchair. It was the sort of thing that at one time would have had them both helpless with laughter, but the laughter had stopped when Tom died and when he very nearly followed him.

'Fine,' she'd said hotly. 'Then hurry up and go. I can't wait.'

Those were the words he'd wanted to hear — yet at the same time, the words that broke his heart.

'I couldn't bear it,' she said now, back in the present. 'I knew I couldn't go through that again. I know it was selfish to want you to give it up, but I didn't think I could live with the fear of losing you.'

But she'd lost him anyway. What an idiot he'd been back then. But they'd both been grappling with shock at what had happened. He'd been a self-pitying fool. All he could see ahead of them was months of physiotherapy and the distinct possibility that life as he knew it would have to change and he had a partner who seemed hell-bent on pushing him into change he didn't want to contemplate. If he'd agreed to give up the RNLI, it would have felt like giving up on his life as he knew it.

They'd warned him he might never walk again and he'd been determined to prove them wrong, but part of him — a very loud, insistent part — kept asking, 'What if?'

And now he saw it from her perspective, where the only thing she could see in their future was a vision of herself at his graveside with the ghosts of the children they would never have. They'd both been struggling with feelings neither of them knew how to handle and instead of it bringing them together, it had blown them apart.

'I should have been more understanding,' he said. 'I don't think I once considered the effect it all had on you. Not the immediate effect, anyway.'

'And what was I thinking?' she said. 'Laying the law down about your future when you were struggling to get out of that wheelchair? I had no right.'

He pulled her closer and there was a short silence before she pulled away. 'What a night,' she said. 'How did I end up in your bed?'

'You don't remember falling asleep in the bath?'

'Did I?'

'I woke you up. You put yourself to bed, but I don't think you were really with it.'

'Right,' she said, chewing the inside of her cheek. She remembered having a nightmare about finding Georgie on the beach, and a violent shudder shook her body. It had been horrible. So vivid. She remembered Bram coming in and holding her. Then another nightmare. The whole night was a confused mess.

'You stayed with me?' she said.

'I couldn't leave you. The nightmares . . .'

'No, of course not.' She smiled nervously. 'You couldn't have woken me up and sent me home?'

'An elephant could have jumped in the bed with you and you'd have slept through,' he said. 'You were well and truly out of it. I put some dressings on your scratches and grazes.'

'Thank you.'

'Would you like me to go?'

'I think that would be best.'

The nightmare — the first one. It was still there. Still in her head. It hadn't been Georgie they'd found on the beach, but it could have been. And then she saw him again, as vividly as if she was still holding him in her arms. That poor little boy.

'Do you feel okay?' he said. 'You keep shivering.'

'I can't stop thinking about . . . '

'I know,' he said, and once again he drew her into his embrace. This time she was wide awake as she snuggled into him.

He bent his head and kissed her. It was meant to be a soft, brief kiss of reassurance, but her lips parted with a soft sigh and the kiss became deeper. He held back, almost expecting her to start hitting him again, but she wound her arms round him and pulled him closer.

'Don't leave me, Bram,' she murmured. 'Don't let me go to sleep again.'

'I'm here,' he said. 'For as long as you want me. I'm here.' He meant it too. He ached for her and at that moment, he would have been happy to stay like this forever, just holding her in his arms. 'But you must sleep. You need it.'

'I need to go home,' she argued; then she yawned. 'I'll just gather my thoughts, then I'll go.'

Two minutes later she fell deeply asleep with her head on his chest: proper sleep this time, untroubled by dreams.

Bram woke first, gently moved Regan off his chest and slipped out of bed. When he returned with coffee, she was just waking up. She yawned and stretched and smiled up at him. Relief flooded through him, then she sat up looking shocked.

'It's morning!' she cried. 'I've been here all night?'

'Is that a problem?' he said, suddenly seized with the fear that it was a problem for her — a big, insurmountable problem.

She slumped back against the pillows.

'It's not a problem,' she said, and smiled. 'Thanks for the coffee. I can't remember the last time I had coffee in bed. In fact, it was probably . . . ' Her eyes darkened. 'I think the last time was when you made it for me.'

'You're not mad about spending the night, are you?' he said.

'No.' She picked up her cup and smiled at him over the rim, but then it was back — that strange look in her eyes as if something had just dawned on her, some awful truth. It was as if she was keeping something from him. He wondered if there was someone else, someone significant in her life. It was ridiculous to hope or even think that she'd lived the life of a nun for the past six years. She was a beautiful woman.

'Have a shower, then we'll have breakfast,' he said. 'I can run you home before surgery so you can grab a change of clothes, then maybe we could have lunch.'

'Whoa!' she said. 'Hold your horses, Bram. Lunch?'

'Just lunch,' he said. 'Now I've found you again, I don't want to waste a moment.'

'I can't,' she said. 'Not today. And I'd rather walk home. I need to clear my head. I have a lot to think about.'

'I understand that, but it's raining.'

'I've been wet before.'

'You are one annoying woman, do you know that? Why are you holding back, Regan? Do you remember kissing me last night?'

She reached out and squeezed his hand. 'We need to talk, Bram. There are things we have to get straight between us. Six years is a long time. Things happen. Circumstances change.'

He nodded. She was right of course. They couldn't just leap straight back into a relationship after all this time. They were different people now. He liked to think he was anyway. 'I put your clothes in the machine last night. They should be dry, but they'll need ironing. I'm hopeless at ironing.'

'Some things never change.'

'How true that is.'

When he came back with her clothes, she was standing at the window wearing his dressing gown, looking down at the camper van that had been his home for so long.

'Come and have breakfast,' he said. 'I make great scrambled eggs on toast.'

'Really?'

'Yeah,' he said. 'I learned to cook properly. I don't live on microwave meals these days.'

'I've missed this,' Regan said. 'Breakfast with you. You always made great coffee.' Not just breakfast. She'd missed him more than she had ever been able to admit to herself. Last night it all came home to her exactly what she'd lost. She'd considered telling him about Georgie when she woke up, but needed a clear head. It wasn't something she could just blurt out.

And then looking out this morning at that camper van . . . Thinking of him living in that had made her so sad. It wasn't a proper home, and he'd had such a rotten childhood . . . If anyone deserved a decent, loving home, it was him. And he was here now, in this cosy flat — but still alone.

'I didn't realise how hungry I was. I honestly can't remember when I last ate,' she said.

'No wonder you flaked out after half a glass of wine,' he said. 'But seriously, are you feeling okay now? I mean you look okay — more than okay. You look gorgeous.'

He'd always been able to make her feel good about herself, even when she knew she wasn't looking her best. She had no make-up on and her clothes were crumpled. No way could she look gorgeous; yet to him, it seemed, she did.

'The nightmares were bad, Bram,' she said. 'The first one — I dreamt we found Georgie on the beach. It was very real.'

'And perfectly understandable that you mixed the two children up in your mind,' he said. 'It's tragic for all concerned. She's a lovely kid. I hope her parents realise just how special she is.'

'Oh they do,' Regan said. And this was it. Her chance to tell him: *Oh, by the way, Bram, you are one of her parents — isn't that great?* But the words clogged in her throat. She couldn't get them out. Yet she couldn't keep putting it off. If she didn't tell him, someone else would, and soon. But how? How did you tell someone they had a five-year-old daughter?

'I'd really like to meet them,' he said. 'But I probably will if they bring her down to the lifeboat station. She's been promised a look around and maybe a trip out on one of the boats.'

'She'll love that.'

'What kid wouldn't?'

'Exactly.' Regan took a deep breath. She hadn't had time to prepare what she was going to say, but the best way was going to be to come out with it. 'About Georgie,' she began.

'Yeah?'

'She's — '

The phone rang. 'Excuse me,' he said. 'Sorry.'

Saved by the bell. Regan wasn't sure whether to be relieved or annoyed. She'd been about to tell him, and the moment had been snatched away.

'I'm so sorry, Regan,' he said. 'I've got to go out. An emergency. Difficult foaling. Will you wait?'

'I can't,' she said. 'But I'll see you later. Go on, go! I'll clear up here.'

He grabbed her by the arms and kissed her on the mouth. She could still feel the pressure of his lips on hers long after she heard his car drive away.

Despite what she'd said about not waiting, Bram hoped she'd still be there when he got home, but of course she'd gone. She'd loaded up the dishwasher, tidied up and made the bed.

He realised he still didn't know where she lived, so he couldn't call round to see her or phone her. Damn. But last night had meant something to her. She'd get back in touch with him.

She knew where he was.

He had a full day at the surgery ahead and he had to get on with it and not think about Regan or whatever it was she was about to tell him. Something about Georgie? Maybe she knew the mother. Or perhaps she was going to tell him to back off and stop getting so involved. That was more likely. She always used to say he got too intense about things. But Regan was different now. She seemed more understanding. And when it came to getting involved, well, she seemed to have done that herself. Big-time.

He was likely to meet Georgie's mum this morning. Bonnie had an appointment at ten. But when the time came, it was Lally who brought the dog in. Bram made a fuss of her and marvelled at the resilience of animals. She greeted him like a long-lost friend and he was very happy with her. 'She seems fine,' he said. 'How's Georgie?'

'I believe she's going to come home today after the doctor has seen her.

That's why I brought Bonnie in. Her mum's at the hospital.'

'Of course,' he said.

'She was very adamant about paying you,' Lally said.

'And I'm adamant that she has enough on her plate without worrying about vet bills. Anyway, she didn't bring her in and ask for treatment. I took it upon myself to give it. That lets her off, don't you think?'

Lally laughed. 'Oh, you are lovely, aren't you? That's so kind. Things haven't been easy for her. If she'd lost Georgie . . . ' Her eyes filled up. 'But she didn't,' she added quickly. 'And we must look at it that way. There is nothing we can do for that other poor little soul, but we still have Georgie.'

'Is she on her own — Georgie's mother?'

Lally gave him a long look as if considering how much to tell him. In the end she smiled and touched his arm. 'Oh, yes, completely on her own,' she said. 'And she's a wonderful mother. From

183

what I gather, her parents moved away just after Georgie was born. They weren't a very close family I'm afraid. I think her mother was so worried she might be called upon to help out with a bit of babysitting, that she took fright and left the country.' Lally's lips tightened with disapproval.

'Really?' Bram was shocked and a little disgusted. 'Their loss, don't you think?'

'Oh, most definitely. But their loss is my gain. I'm Georgie's sort-of honorary grandmother. I look after her when . . .' She hesitated. 'When her mum is at work. I used to baby-sit for little Jay sometimes too.' Her eyes clouded. 'I'm very lucky that I moved in near them when I did. This is a lovely little community.'

'Yes, it is. You're not from around here?'

'Goodness, no,' she said. 'My husband and I used to come here on holiday sometimes. We stayed at a B&B on the front and we often used to say we'd like to retire here. Sadly it wasn't to be.'

Again her eyes misted, but she smiled quickly. This was a woman used to picking herself up, Bram thought.

'I'm sorry,' he said. It was a shame. She seemed such a nice person. He liked her a lot.

'Don't be,' she said. 'I could have stayed where I was and felt sorry for myself, but I decided to hell with it and I made the move. I've never looked back. It's a lovely place to live, isn't it? But you're not a local either, are you?'

'No,' he said. 'I lived here for a while a few years ago and it got to me the same way it got to you. I had to come back.'

But in his case it wasn't just the town, it was Regan; and it was turning out to be the most sensible decision he'd ever made in his life. He only wished he'd come back sooner instead of wasting so many years licking his wounds.

10

It was so good to have Bonnie and Georgie back home. Regan kept looking at them and wanting to pinch herself to prove it was real. Georgie was a little subdued, but that was only natural after all she'd been through.

There was last night too. That felt unreal already, as if it had happened a long time ago.

'Mummy, Bram said I could go to the lifeboat station. Can we go tomorrow?'

'Tomorrow? Oh, I don't know.'

'You haven't got to go to work, have you?' Georgie had never been a clingy child, but she looked positively distraught at the thought of Regan going to work. Thank goodness she'd been able to book a decent amount of time off.

'No, I've got a few days off,' Regan said. The way she felt right now, she never wanted to go back; never wanted to leave Georgie again. She fondled Bonnie's ears thoughtfully.

Bram would be busy at the surgery tomorrow, so he wouldn't be there. Perhaps it would be better to arrange something sooner rather than later and get it over with. Once that was done, then she could go and see Bram and tell him about Georgie.

She had every intention of telling him that he was a father, but it had to be in her own time and in her own way. She didn't want to spring it on him out of the blue.

Coward, a voice in her mind said.

'I could give Len a ring and ask about tomorrow,' she said.

'Will I be able to go even though my arm's broken?' She lifted her arm and looked at the cast.

'Of course,' Regan said. 'In fact we should get everyone to sign their names on it. I can get a special pen that will write on it.' Everyone except Bram, of course.

'Call him now, Mummy!'

'All right,' Regan said, picking up the phone.

Len answered on the second ring. 'Hello, love,' he said. 'How's the little one?'

'She's fine,' she said. 'Raring to go.'

'That's good to hear,' he said. 'How about you? How are you bearing up?'

'Me? I'm fine, Len.'

'I take it you haven't spoken to Bram yet?' he said. 'No, of course you haven't. I saw him on the beach with his dogs this morning and he was happier than I've seen him since he got back. But if you'd told him about Georgie, he would have mentioned it I'm sure.'

'He was happy?' she said, feeling ridiculously pleased.

'Very.'

'I will tell him, Len. It's not something I can just spring on him though, is it?'

'I suppose not,' he sighed. 'You know him best. Just don't leave it too long. So what can I do for you, love?'

'Would it be possible to come to the lifeboat station tomorrow so Georgie can say thank you?'

'While Bram is busy at the surgery?' he said with another sigh. 'Well, why not? It'll do Georgie good and after all, the situation between you and Bram is hardly her fault. I'll arrange for someone from the newspaper to come at the same time. We'll get some photos done and it'll give us some publicity. We might get a few donations in.'

'Thank you,' Regan said, feeling like a heel.

'To be honest it seems a bit harsh to leave Bram out, love, if I may say so, considering he saved her life.'

'I know. I feel really bad about this, Len, but I need time to talk to him before he sees us together and figures it out for himself.'

'Bring her down at eleven tomorrow morning. Wear something warm.'

'Thanks, Len.'

'But Regan, I want your word that you'll talk to him. Soon.'

'You have it.'

She hung up. She had to stop feeling guilty about all this. Bram was the one who vanished off the face of the earth, not her! He could have come back any time.

'Mummy?'

'Tomorrow morning,' she said, cuddling Georgie up against her. 'How exciting is that?'

Regan's next call was to her parents, who had retired to an apartment in Spain. They'd seen Georgie no more than half a dozen times, but Regan felt duty-bound to tell them what had happened. They'd never been a close family, but she always hoped that having a grandchild would give them a second chance. They hadn't wanted it, though, and if it hadn't been for lovely Lally turning up when she had, Regan didn't know what she would have done.

'You see, Regan,' Lilian said when Regan had finished talking, 'This is precisely why I didn't want to get involved.' She hadn't seemed to notice

190

the catch in Regan's voice or that she was struggling not to cry as she recounted the tragic events. If it had been Georgie on the other end of the phone, Regan thought, she would have moved heaven and earth to get to her and comfort her. But Lilian was her usual cool, detached self.

'It's a pretty poor reason,' Regan muttered, and Lilian sighed heavily.

'You were just the same as a child, always running wild.'

'Georgie was not running wild!' Oh why on earth did she bother? What was she expecting? Sympathy? Understanding? She held tight to the phone, fighting the urge to just hang up.

'She had to be rescued from the cliff in the middle of the night while you were at work,' Lilian said. 'If that's not running wild I don't know what is. And you say this other child died? How dreadful. I'm so sorry.'

'Yes. I found him.'

'Hold on, darling. Your father wants to speak to you.'

There was a brief clattering at the other end of the line as the phone changed hands. 'Are you all right, love?' he said. 'I got the gist of it from your mother's side of the conversation. Is Georgie okay?'

'She'll mend,' Regan said. 'She's very shaken.'

'As you must be too,' he said, and the kindness in his voice almost had her in tears. She'd always been closer to him than to her mother. 'Would you like me to come over for a while? Or perhaps you'd like to come out here? The weather is much kinder at the moment. It's lovely and warm.'

'Thank you, that's very sweet of you.' It was the first time her parents had invited her out to Spain. She could imagine her mother pulling faces at him, urging him not to press the matter. 'But we're all right. Lally is helping a lot.'

'Lally? Oh, the child-minder woman.'

'She's my friend, Dad,' Regan said, angered by his dismissive tone. 'I don't know how I'd manage without her to be honest.'

'Good, good,' he said, and she could feel him withdrawing from her. 'Did I tell you how warm it is here? We've had wall-to-wall sunshine for days.'

'Yes, Dad, you did.'

'So glad we made the move out here,' he went on. 'We're so happy here, far away from all our troubles.'

'Troubles?' Did he mean her? Was that how her parents saw her?

'The weather and so on,' he said. 'Not you. Heavens no. I didn't mean that.' She had always felt slightly in the way, as if her parents hadn't really wanted her. Once she'd asked her mum why she didn't have any brothers or sisters and Lilian had replied, 'We weren't going to make that mistake again.' As a teenager, it wasn't Regan who was desperate to grow up and leave home, but her parents who were eager for her to do so. And when she did leave home, they wasted no time in converting her bedroom into a study for her dad, making it absolutely clear she wasn't coming back.

'Sorry to have disturbed you, Dad,' she said.

'We're always glad to hear from you, love,' he said. 'You know that. Take care. Love you.'

'Love you too,' she said. She supposed her parents did love her in their way.

She looked at Georgie as she hung up. She would never, ever, let her little girl feel anything other than cherished. And she was certainly never going to let her think she was a mistake. Her only mistake had been in not tracking Bram down and making them into a proper family. Love had no bounds. She knew that. It didn't have to be limited to two people.

Len was waiting for them at the lifeboat station and there were several other guys there that Regan recognised. Malcolm came over and shook her hand.

'Shame Bram couldn't make it,' he

said. 'He's busy at the surgery. I suppose you had to fit this in around your job at the hospital.'

She avoided his eyes. He knew! 'Yes,' she muttered guiltily. *Liar!*

They made a huge fuss of Georgie before they donned lifejackets and were taken out in the small boat. Georgie was tremendously excited and Regan kept her close, terrified in case she fell overboard even though she was perfectly safe on board. It was a calm day and thank goodness the sea was flat. They went along the coast so Georgie could watch seals basking in the sun on a sand bar.

'She has her father's eyes,' Len remarked, and Regan glared at him. 'Just saying.' He shrugged. 'If I can see it, it's only a matter of time before . . . '

'Len!' Regan said. She knew what he was going to say. It was only a matter of time before Bram looked in the mirror and realised Georgie's eyes were looking right back at him.

'I'm going to work on the lifeboat

when I'm big,' Georgie said. 'Like my daddy.'

Len gave Regan a questioning look.

'Georgie knows what kind of man her father is,' she explained.

'He's a hero,' Georgie said. 'Like Bram.'

Those words were like a knife in Regan's heart. This deception had gone on long enough. It wasn't just Bram she was deceiving, but Georgie too. This brave little girl had every right to know who her father was and Regan had no doubt that Bram would be a wonderful father. The only thing holding her back now was the fear of how he would feel about her once the truth was out. And that was selfish in the extreme.

When they got back, a woman from the local paper was waiting with a photographer. Regan kept out of the photos as Georgie posed with the lifeboat men. Then the woman asked the question: 'Which one of you went over the cliff and saved her?'

'He's not here,' Len said.

And then it all happened. 'Yes he is,' Malcolm said, and Regan looked up to see Bram striding down the path towards them, his dogs running at his heels. His hair shone like gold in the sunshine and the slightly puzzled look on his face nearly broke her heart. He was wearing jeans and his leather jacket, and the sight of him made her heart flip and her stomach clench. Desire and fear all mingled together inside. She sank back, wishing the shadows would gobble her up, but Rags had spotted her and hurtled towards her, greeting her like a long-lost friend.

'Oh, no,' she groaned as she stooped to make a fuss of the little dog. 'Not now. Not like this.'

His face lit up when he saw her. It was unbearable. She was going to hurt him — badly. If only he didn't look so pleased to see her. So happy.

'Have I missed all the fun?' he asked lightly. 'I got down here as soon as I could after surgery.'

'Hello, Bram!' Georgie piped up.

'Hi, Georgie,' Bram said, and he picked her up as if she weighed nothing at all, being careful of her arm. 'Where have you been? Out on the boat?'

'Yes, we went out on the sea,' Georgie said, eyes sparkling. 'It was fantastic!'

'I bet it was,' Bram said, and his forehead crinkled slightly. He looked around, obviously looking for Georgie's mother.

'Bram . . . ' Regan began, but it was too late. The trouble she'd been so worried about was now rolling down the hill and picking up speed. There was no way back now. It was unstoppable. Bram was going to find out in the most horrible way imaginable, right here in front of loads of people.

'Bram's the guy who rescued Georgie,' Len said with an unhappy look at Regan. 'I'm sorry,' he mouthed, but she knew if he hadn't pointed it out, someone else would have done.

'Great,' the reporter said. 'We'll get a picture of the two of you together.

Actually, let's have Mum in it too.' She waved her hand at Regan. Bram looked around, again looking for 'mum'; and as Regan stepped forward, she saw realisation dawn on his face. He frowned, then looked at Georgie, then Regan. One by one, he looked at the faces of his fellow crew members. Some knew, some didn't. But Bram knew now. He had to. Malcolm rested his hand on Bram's shoulder and whispered that he was sorry, and Bram's expression darkened.

'Come on, Mummy,' Georgie urged, pulling her over to stand beside Bram.

'Is this some kind of joke?' he whispered.

'I'm sorry,' Regan said. 'I tried to tell you.'

'Oh, you did? I must have missed that! I mean, exactly when did you try to tell me that Georgie was your child?'

Oh God, he still didn't know. It was only a matter of time before the penny finished dropping. Then what? Would he storm off? And what effect would all this have on Georgie?

'What did you take me for? Why didn't you tell me? And where's her father?'

'Over here, please,' the photographer called out.

'All right, honey?' Bram spoke to Georgie. As far as she was concerned, he was all warmth as he squatted down beside her and put his arm around her. 'You feeling okay?'

'Yes, thank you. Will you write your name on my cast too? Everyone else has.'

'Sure I will,' he said. 'Is there any room left? Did you leave a space for me?'

'Yes,' she giggled. 'Mummy gave me a special pen. It's in my pocket.'

Bram couldn't believe the child was Regan's; but now that he knew, of course he could see it. She had the same colour of hair like thick, rich chocolate. Those stunning blue eyes weren't from Regan though. So there must be someone else in her life, although Lally said Georgie's mother was on her own. So who . . .

'How old are you again?' he said.

'Five and a half,' Georgie said.

You didn't have to be a mathematical genius to figure it out. He looked into those eyes, a mirror of his own, and it was as if someone had smashed his ribs apart and wrenched out his heart. If he believed such things were possible, he would have said he felt it break in two.

11

His daughter. His child. His and Regan's, and he hadn't had a clue. And if he hadn't come back when he did, he might never have found out. This child, this beautiful little girl, would have grown up never knowing she had a father who would have loved her. Correction — who would love her. No wonder he'd felt a connection.

He couldn't bring himself to look at Regan. He didn't trust himself. He'd missed five years of his daughter's life. Five important, crucial years. A lifetime. Georgie's lifetime. He'd been denied the chance to sit up with her in the wee small hours. He knew how precious that quiet time at night was for a parent and child. It was a time for quiet reflection and bonding. And her first steps, first words, first tooth, first day at school — so many firsts had been stolen from him.

How had he not seen it? Back at the hospital, when Regan was sitting outside the ward . . . It had been handed to him on a plate. When he'd gone in to see Georgie, what had she said? Something like, 'You just missed my mum. She only left a little while ago . . . ' How could he have been so blind? So stupid? It was easy now, with hindsight, to put two and two together, but back then he hadn't even had an inkling.

'Smile please,' the photographer said. Bram looked down at Georgie and his smile was genuine. His daughter. His child. Little wonder she felt so special to him. He looked away for a moment and caught Regan's eye. She looked terrified, as well she might.

If she thought he was going to step back and stay out of their lives, she had another thing coming. Georgie was his daughter and he was going to be a father to her whether Regan liked it or not.

He almost hated her. Almost. But even now, he couldn't bring himself to hate her. And what had Lally said? Something about her parents moving abroad? Typical of them. They'd never seemed very interested in their daughter's life. It was almost as if she'd been an inconvenience. But this wasn't about feeling sorry for Regan. Her past had no bearing on the present.

Surely she didn't think she could keep this from him? Someone would have said something eventually. And she'd had plenty of opportunity to tell him. Hell, they'd spent a whole night together! He shook his head and she cast her eyes down.

Pretending that everything was fine was one of the hardest things he'd ever had to do — harder than fighting stormy seas or climbing down cliffs or being lowered from a helicopter into a swirling storm.

The people from the press left, happy with their photos, and some of the guys headed off. In the end it just left Bram and Len with Georgie and Regan, and he had the feeling Len was only hanging around to act as peacekeeper, just in case full-scale war broke out.

Len. He must have known. And Malcolm. Did everyone know apart from him? But Bram wasn't about to start anything in front of this — his — little girl.

'I'll make some tea,' Len said. 'Would you like to come with me, Georgie? Your mummy and Bram can walk along the beach with the dogs and you can watch the boats through my binoculars.'

'Yay!' Georgie said. Bram could barely stop looking at her, as if he wanted to soak her up and try to fill in all that he'd missed.

'And I've probably got some biscuits. That all right, Regan?' She smiled and nodded.

Bram set off ahead of her across the sand, the dogs charging about around him, chasing each other and sending protesting geese into the air. She had to run to catch up with him. 'I know what you're thinking,' she said.

He stopped and glared down at her. He wanted to grab her by the shoulders and shake her till her teeth rattled. 'Don't kid yourself. You have absolutely no idea what I'm thinking,' he said stonily. Probably just as well. His thoughts were pretty murderous, and the hurt was like nothing he'd ever felt before.

'I think I do,' she said. 'Please, let me explain.'

'What's to explain? You split up with me when you were pregnant and didn't even give me the chance . . . ' He broke off. God, this was painful. 'You didn't give me the chance to be a father to my child.'

'I'm sorry.' She hung her head and he turned away from her and started walking again. Once more she ran to catch up. 'Bram, please . . . '

'Just know this, Regan,' he said. 'Georgie is my daughter and I want to be a proper father to her. And that means you giving up work for a start.'

'What? Are you insane? I'm doing no such thing.' That had stopped her in her tracks.

'No? Hard isn't it, being asked to give up something that's in your blood?' She looked stunned. 'But you will give up working nights.'

'Oh, will I?' She'd never taken to being told what to do. She was like him in that respect.

'With my support you can cut your hours and be home for Georgie more.'

'Your support?'

'Financial support,' he spelled it out for her. 'Don't worry, I'm not going to force you to marry me or anything stupid like that. I think that ship vanished over the horizon some time ago, don't you?'

He waited for her to argue. This wasn't like Regan at all, standing there silently, letting him call the shots. He felt wrong-footed, but hey, he was the wronged party here, not her. He'd done pussyfooting around. 'I want time with my daughter,' he went on. 'I want to get

to know her and to be part of her life.'
He turned away from her, because it
was hard to keep this up with her
standing there looking so small and
vulnerable. It was not a look he was
used to when it came to Regan. It
would be better if she argued with him
and flung around a few accusations so
he could at least fire back with some
anger. As it was, his anger was
beginning to fade and bewilderment
was taking its place.

'I don't understand,' he said. 'You
know the kind of childhood I had. I
know not all single parents are as
useless as my father was, but if it hadn't
been for my grandparents, God knows
where I'd have ended up. And what's
Georgie got? Just you . . . you and a
neighbour. What if something happened
to you, Regan? Would your parents
come back and take care of her?'

'Nothing's going to happen to me,'
she said quietly.

'I'm sure that's exactly what my
mother thought before she was run

down and killed.' He closed his eyes. He'd always vowed that when he had kids, they weren't going to have the sort of unhappy, insecure childhood he'd had. And it would have been so much worse without his grandparents. Georgie didn't even have that.

Regan had never heard Bram speak so openly or so bitterly about his childhood before. She knew he'd lost his mother at an early age and that his father had struggled to bring him up alone. But he was right! Somewhere in all that, he'd touched a nerve. She was alone. Very alone. It wasn't something she'd ever allowed herself to think about. She couldn't bear to look at Bram and see the hurt in his eyes, hurt that she'd put there.

'What would have happened if I hadn't come back?' he asked.

'I don't know. I've often thought of trying to contact you, but it's been six years, Bram. I thought you might be married with children by now. I was about to tell you yesterday morning, but then you were called out on an emergency. This has all happened so fast. I didn't even know you were back until you came into the hospital.' She hoped he'd understand how difficult this was for her.

'You're unbelievable, do you know that?' he said.

'If it's any consolation, I don't like myself very much right now, Bram. If you knew how many times I've wanted to find you . . . '

'Well, you didn't try very hard did you?'

'I didn't try at all,' she said. 'That's the truth of it. But even if I'd wanted to, I wouldn't have known where to start. I wasn't the one who ran away.'

'I didn't run away! You told me to go, remember? So what did you tell Georgie? She must have asked questions. Did you tell her I'd died?'

Regan drew in her breath. 'I told her you loved her very much, but that you had to go away. I . . . I said I'd explain it to her properly when she was older.

She knows her father is a lifeboat man and very brave.' He looked surprised. 'I will tell her about you,' she went on. 'But not right now. She's had a lot to deal with.'

'Okay.'

'You're all right with that? You won't say anything to her?'

He laughed bitterly. 'What do you take me for, Regan? You really don't know me at all, do you?'

'It seems not,' she murmured.

Georgie trained the binoculars on her mum and Bram. 'Bram's got loads of dogs, hasn't he?' she said.

'Yes,' Len chuckled.

'He looks very cross. Why is he so angry?'

Len took the binoculars. 'Let me see,' he said. 'Oh, wait, look out there. Is that a pirate ship?' He passed them back to her and while her attention was diverted he looked along the beach.

'That's not a pirate ship, Uncle Len,' she giggled.

Bram certainly did look angry. Even

from this distance, the body language was loud and clear. Len felt sorry for them both. Regan looked small and hunched, like a child being told off. Len tried to imagine how he'd feel. He'd never had kids, but if he had, he would have been devastated to have been kept out of their lives. His wife, Molly, had died several years ago and his one sadness was that they didn't have children. It wasn't for want of trying. They both would have loved a big family, but it wasn't to be. And there were those two with the makings of a lovely little family, and the tragedy was they seemed to hate each other.

Suddenly Bram's arms dropped to his sides and he hung his head. Regan reached out to him as if she was going to touch him, but changed her mind and shoved her hands in her pockets.

They turned back, walking together but miles apart, the dogs bouncing around them. If they'd only see sense and get together. It wasn't too late. Bram was bound to be angry. In fact, angry probably didn't cover it. They were both strong, proud, stubborn people. He couldn't see this having a happy ending, no matter how much he wished for it. 'Shame,' he murmured. 'Dirty rotten shame.' He looked down and Georgie was looking up at him.

'What is?' she asked.

He sighed. 'Nothing, sweetie,' he said.

'Can we make a cup of tea for Bram and Mummy?' she said.

'I think that would be a great idea.' He grinned. 'I'll boil the kettle and you put the sugar in the mugs. We'll put plenty in; see if we can sweeten them up a little.'

'Tea?' Bram said. 'But I . . .'

'Georgie helped make it,' Len said quickly.

'Well in that case,' Bram said, 'how can I refuse?'

They sat down around a small table. Regan was on edge. Despite what Bram had said, she was afraid something would be said. This was such a delicate situation. The only one who seemed completely unaware of all the tension sparking around them was Georgie. Even the dogs seemed unsettled and restless.

Regan had been mortified at first when she saw Bram coming, knowing that the truth was about to come out. But now she'd got over the shock, she started to feel angry. Yes, angry! It was all very well him acting all wounded and wronged, but it wasn't completely down to her. She knew only too well how it felt to be unwanted. Oh, her parents had given her everything she needed. They'd fed her, clothed her, made sure she got to school on time, but it was always clear they were biding their time, counting off the years until they 'got their lives back,' as they put it. And they saw nothing wrong in it! It was the way they were. Regan's birth was unplanned and unwelcome and while Georgie's birth was unplanned, Regan had wanted the baby with all her heart and soul from the minute she knew she was there.

How could she risk chasing Bram and telling him he was about to become a father? They'd made a clean break. They'd agreed to split up. He might have ended up feeling trapped, and ultimately Georgie would have been the one to suffer. And no child should ever feel unwanted. *No*, she thought, *I did nothing wrong. I did what I thought was right.*

Georgie offered her the biscuit tin and she took one. Then she offered it to Bram.

'Thanks, honey,' he said and winked, making the little girl giggle.

Hah, charm on legs, Regan thought, but when he looked her way, his smile vanished and his eyes hardened. This time she didn't feel swamped with guilt and she held his gaze. Two could play at this game. She lifted her chin and his eyebrows rose fractionally. If he wanted to turn this into a fight, fine!

As soon as Lally saw Regan coming, she knew something terrible had happened. She looked as if she'd been crying again. But Georgie was bouncing along at her side, arm in a sling, happy as Larry.

'What's up?' she called out.

Georgie rushed over, full of herself. 'I've been out on a boat and saw the seals and Uncle Len let me use his binoculars and I saw a big boat and we had our photos taken . . .'

'Steady on, don't forget to breathe,' Lally laughed.

'We made tea for Mummy and Bram and Bram's got hundreds of dogs and they went for a walk on the beach and Bram was cross and Mummy was waving her arms about . . .'

Regan nearly choked. 'What's that, Miss?' she said.

'I saw you. And Uncle Len said it was a dirty rotten shame.'

'What was?' Regan seemed perilously close to cracking up. Her voice had gone very shrill.

'I don't know.' Georgie shrugged.

'Come in,' Lally said. 'I'll put the

216

kettle on. I think you need to tell me what's been going on.'

'Georgie just did,' Regan said with a sigh. 'We went down to the lifeboat station.'

'Yes, I know that. I want to hear the rest. I want to know what's a dirty rotten shame.'

'Everything,' Regan sighed.

'Look at my cast,' Georgie said. 'Everyone wrote on it, even the lady from the newspaper.'

'Wow, that's great, Georgie. You'll be able to keep that forever, like an autograph book, but on a cast.'

'What's an autograph book?'

Lally laughed. 'Oh, it's something we all used to have when I was young. You'd get all your friends to write messages in it and sometimes if you were lucky, you'd see someone famous and get them to put their name in too. I got Cliff Richard. I had such a big crush on him.'

'What's a crush?'

Regan was laughing now too. 'Keep

digging, Lally,' she said. 'You're getting yourself in deeper and deeper.'

'I have an idea,' Lally said. 'Follow me, Georgie.' She went into her kitchen and took a box of dry cat food down from the shelf. 'Do me a favour and shake this about a bit around the garden, there's a good girl. See if you can get my cats home.'

'Okay!' Georgie bounded out the back door and began to patrol the garden, shaking the box.

'Let's hope my cats are chasing rats over at Brook's Farm,' Lally said. 'The longer she's out there, the better. So what's going on, Regan?'

'Bram found out today that he's Georgie's father.'

Lally's jaw dropped. 'How? Did you tell him?'

'No. It came out at the lifeboat station in front of about a dozen people. It was awful, Lally.'

Lally covered her mouth with her hand. 'Awful? I should think it was. How did he take it? Judging by the look on your face, not well.'

'I should have told him. It was stupid trying to wait for the right time, because there's never a right time to tell someone something like that, is there? He feels betrayed, humiliated, hurt. Oh God, Lally, so hurt.'

'But Georgie still doesn't know?'

'I don't think it's going to be any easier telling her to be honest.'

Lally looked out of the window. Two of her cats had appeared and were following Georgie round the garden.

'But what can I do, Lally? I can't turn back the clock. And now I have to accept that he wants to be in Georgie's life.' She paced up and down until she made Lally feel dizzy. 'He wants me to give up work, or at least cut my hours, so I can spend more time with Georgie.'

Lally stifled a cheer and nodded. 'That makes sense.' Regan worked far too hard. It would be brilliant if she could spend more time at home with Georgie.

'What? Whose side are you on?'

'How many times have you said you wished you didn't have to work nights?' Lally reminded her.

'I know . . . '

'This could be a good thing, love,' Lally said, rubbing Regan's back as she spoke. It was a comforting, motherly gesture. 'Look on the positive side. This can only be good for Georgie.'

'Until he kills himself.'

'That's unlikely,' Lally said. 'I know what he does is dangerous, but . . . '

'You sound like him.'

'Just saying it like it is, Regan. She's coming back.' Lally opened the back door and Georgie entered, followed by four cats. 'Let's give them some food, then we'll have a drink and you can tell me all about your day.'

Regan sat down and gazed out of the window. Any hopes she'd had of a reconciliation with Bram had blown out of the window. She couldn't see him ever forgiving her for this and in all honesty, she didn't blame him.

12

The following day Regan answered a knock at the door and found Bram standing on the porch. 'How did you..?'

'I know your dog's address even if you refused to give me yours,' he said. 'Hey, Bonnie ... ' The traitorous hound rushed into his arms and he picked her up while she wiggled and squirmed and licked all over his face. 'At least someone's pleased to see me,' he said.

'Bram!' Georgie squealed, and he put the dog down and picked up the little girl.

'Oh, for goodness sake,' Regan muttered. 'You'd better come in.'

There was no choice in the matter. As soon as he put Georgie down, she clasped his hand and dragged him into the cosy sitting room. He looked around. There were pictures of Georgie everywhere. He picked one up of her as a baby and Regan gulped down the lump in her throat when she saw tears shimmering in his eyes.

'She was a lovely baby,' she said, taking the photo from him and putting it back down.

'She looks it,' he said gruffly. 'I bet you felt very proud when you pushed her around in her pram, didn't you?'

'Yes, I . . . ' She sighed. 'I've said I'm sorry. I don't know what more you expect from me.'

'Can Bram stay for tea, Mummy?'

'No,' Regan said.

'I'd love to,' he countered, sitting himself down in the armchair, crossing his long legs and making himself completely at home.

'But you have evening surgery, right?' Regan said.

'Wrong. I'm all finished for the day and I happen to be starving.'

The nerve of him, inviting himself to dinner. Or rather, allowing himself to be invited. He didn't have to accept, but he had, so now her task was to get dinner cooked and over and done with as soon as possible. 'What about your dogs?' she said. 'They'll be all alone.'

'They have each other and besides, I took them for a good run earlier. Don't worry, Regan; everything is under control.'

'I'm not worried,' she said and stormed into the kitchen. As she clattered about preparing dinner, she could hear Bram and Georgie chatting and laughing. She was glad they were getting on so well. It meant when they did start sorting out access, Georgie would be able to spend time with him on her own. It would be nice for Georgie to have a man in her life. And she already loved Bram and she was certainly safe with him. The sooner Regan told their daughter the truth, the better.

'Lally, right?' Len said when he saw the woman standing at her front gate looking anxiously across the road at Regan's house. He saw the cause for her concern. Bram's car was parked outside. 'Oh, dear. I was going to pop in and see her, but perhaps I'd best not,' he said.

'Len, isn't it?' she said, and her face broke into a smile. Her grey hair was caught back in a loose ponytail and when she smiled, her face instantly lost ten years. He'd seen her around town, but never before realised how attractive she was.

'Glad to meet you properly at last.' He grinned back and held out his hand. 'You've been a great friend to Regan and she's really needed a friend these past few years.'

'Why don't you come in?' Lally said.

'Are you sure? I was just planning to see if Regan was okay, but I don't think I should if she has company.'

'I was thinking the same thing,' she said. 'Wondering whether I should pop over. They have a lot to talk about.'

'They certainly do.' Len wondered how much Lally knew about the situation.

'I hope things work out for them,' she

said. 'They'd make such a lovely couple.'

'They used to,' Len said. 'Everyone was amazed when they broke up. It seemed so wrong then, and it still seems wrong now. They should be together. It was meant to be, but frankly the way they're behaving I can't see it happening.' He followed her into the house, sat down on the sofa and almost at once a ginger cat jumped on his lap.

'You don't mind cats, do you?'

'Not in the least.'

'Good,' she said and she gave him a ravishing smile. 'So what are we going to do about Bram and Regan?'

'Do?' Len said. 'Nothing we can do except be around to pick up the pieces when it all blows apart.'

'Or throw confetti when they see sense and get married,' Lally rejoindered.

Len threw back his head and laughed. 'You're a real cup-half-full kind of person, aren't you?' he said.

'Half-full?' She winked at him. 'What are you talking about? My cup is always full to the brim.'

The longer Bram stayed, the easier it became. He felt at home here, sitting on Regan's floor, playing a game with Georgie while Bonnie draped herself over his lap. Unfortunately, the same couldn't be said of Regan. She was on edge and nervy. They couldn't go on like this. Georgie would soon start to sense something was up and the very last thing on his agenda was to upset her. He wanted to be a proper father to her and make up for all the time he'd missed.

He'd helped Regan to wash up and she was in the kitchen now, pottering about, doing anything rather than come through here. If she couldn't even bear to be in the same room as him, it didn't bode well for the future.

Suddenly she appeared in the doorway. Her face was white.

'What is it?'

'Your pager . . . You left it in the kitchen. You've had a shout.'

'Thanks.' He jumped to his feet. 'Thank you for a lovely evening,' he said, and he stooped to kiss Georgie's forehead. 'I've had a brilliant time. Next time you must come to mine and meet my dogs.'

'Can we bring Bonnie?' Georgie asked.

'Of course you can. The more the merrier. Bonnie should get to know my lot anyway.'

Regan saw him to the door. 'Bonnie should get to know your lot?' she said. 'Why? Are you planning on taking my dog too?'

'What? Who said anything about taking anyone? I just thought if we're going to be seeing a lot of each other, it makes sense that our dogs should meet up too.'

'Okay. Just . . . Be careful, Bram. Georgie's already lost her best friend; I don't want her to lose you too.'

As he was leaving, they saw Len rushing out of Lally's house. 'Hey, Bram!' he yelled. 'Can you give me a lift?'

'Sure,' Bram said. Moments later they were gone and Lally was hurrying across the road, holding her cardigan tightly around herself.

'Len?' Regan said quizzically.

'Oh, don't you go reading anything into it. He was on his way to visit you and saw Bram's car and didn't want to interrupt, that's all. I felt sorry for him having walked all the way here, so I made him a cuppa.'

'Hm,' Regan said, stroking her chin. 'I see.'

'No, you don't,' Lally protested. 'There's nothing for you to see. We've only just met properly for heaven's sake.'

'In all the time I've known you, I've never seen you blush before, Lally,' Regan said.

'I'm not!' Lally cried, slapping her hands against her face. 'It's the cold, that's all. Anyway, I came over to see how you are. How did it go? Bram was here for ages. Have you told Georgie?'

'Told me what?' Georgie piped up from behind Regan and Lally bit hard on her lip. 'Oh heck, Regan,' she said. 'Sorry. Should have realised little pigs have big ears.'

Georgie burst out laughing. 'Grown-ups say weird things,' she said and went back inside.

'I'm going to talk to her now,' Regan said. 'I'd planned to anyway. I don't want her to hear from someone else. You know what kids are like. Someone's mum or dad will have heard something now the rumour mill is in motion.'

'I'll leave you to it then,' Lally said. 'Good luck.'

'I'm going to need it,' Regan said with a rueful smile.

★ ★ ★

'So,' Len said. 'You and Regan . . .'

'There is no me and Regan,' Bram replied through clenched teeth.

'Lally said you'd been there a while.'

'I was visiting my daughter who, by the way, you forgot to tell me about.'

'Wasn't my place,' Len said. 'And besides, I didn't realise the kid you rescued was Georgie until later.'

'But you did know about her, right?

Everyone did, bar me.' Bram took his eye off the road for a moment and looked at Len.

'Not everyone, Bram,' Len said. 'You know Regan. Keeps things close to her chest.'

'Did Dennis know?'

'Probably.'

'I just don't get why no one told me.'

'Everyone knew you'd split up. And after you broke up, it wouldn't have seemed right to get you back. You know what Regan's like. Always been independent and self-sufficient. Had to be. And by the time it became obvious she was pregnant, you were long gone.'

Bram knew he could blame everyone else till the cows came home, but at the bottom of it all, he was the one at fault. 'So,' he said with a grin. 'You and Lally . . .'

'What?' Len said, but he couldn't stop a smile. 'I've only just met the woman.'

'She's lovely,' Bram said. 'I like her very much and she's about your age. Single too, I gather.'

'All right,' Len said. 'Point taken. I won't say any more about Regan.'

'It's a bit different, Len,' Bram said. 'There's nothing to stop you and Lally getting together. Truly, I'm happy for you.'

* * *

Georgie looked up at Regan. 'Am I in trouble, Mummy?'

'No, you're not in trouble. Far from it. But I have something to tell you. Something very important.' Georgie nodded. 'It's about your daddy. Remember I told you he was a lifeboat man?'

'Like Bram?'

'Exactly like Bram. Well, Mummy and Daddy loved each other very much, but he had to go away. Sweetie, he's come back and he wants to get to know you.'

'Oh.' Georgie looked thoughtful for a moment. 'Is he going to live here with us?'

'He has his own house, darling,' Regan said.

Georgie looked at her with Bram's eyes. 'Is it Bram?'

Regan couldn't believe it. How could Georgie have guessed? Had someone already said something? She caught her breath. 'Yes, it is,' she said.

'Oh, good.' A smile lit up Georgie's face. 'I really wished he was my daddy, and he is.'

Regan blinked. That had been way too easy. She waited, holding her breath. Something would go wrong here.

'Do you still love him?' Georgie asked.

It was impossible to lie. 'Yes,' Regan said.

'And does that mean all his dogs are our dogs too?' Regan laughed. 'Sort of.'

'Yay! Will we go and live with him?'

'No,' Regan answered quickly. 'But you will be able to visit him.' She couldn't believe how easy that was. If only Bram had taken the news so well.

★   ★   ★

Regan went to Jay's funeral alone. It was heart-breaking. Katie was completely crushed, as if she'd been chewed up and spat out by some monster. She had requested that Regan should say a few words, and it was one of the most difficult things she'd ever had to do.

She'd never felt as alone as she did when she stood at the front of the packed church. Her legs felt weak and she was sure her voice would be thin and shaky, but the words came and she pretended that she was alone in the church with Jay's mother, and her words were just for her. She spoke of Jay's friendship with Georgie and how he'd taken the little girl under his wing at school. He was a very special little boy, very kind and thoughtful.

Jay's dad was there, white-faced, sitting beside Katie, but the two of them might as well have been a hundred miles apart. Regan wanted to hug them both. They needed each other right now. Past differences and hurts should be forgotten, but the tie that had held them together had now gone. There would be no more access visits. Their marriage was truly at an end now, which was so sad when Jay had died in his attempt to force them back together.

The service was mercifully short, and afterwards Katie approached Regan and without a word, wrapped her arms around her and hugged her. 'I'm glad it was you that found him,' she said. 'Jay liked you.'

Regan held her tight. She couldn't stop the tears. 'I'm glad too,' she said. 'I just wish . . . '

'I know, Regan. Thank you.'

When everyone had left, Regan stayed behind and sat in the quiet church. She'd never been to the funeral of a child before and she just needed time alone with her thoughts. She heard the squeak of footsteps on the polished floor and felt someone sit in the same pew. When she turned to look, it was Bram. He was wearing a black suit.

'You're too late,' she said. 'The funeral is over.'

'I know. I was here,' he said. 'Standing at the back. I thought what you said was really nice.'

'Thanks,' she said. 'It wasn't easy.'

'No,' he said. 'It wouldn't be.'

'I'd better go,' she said. 'Georgie will be waiting.'

'Don't leave on my account. I didn't mean to intrude.'

'No, it's time I left anyway.'

He stood so she could pass and as she left the church, she glanced back and saw him sitting down again, head bowed. Some silly part of her wanted to rush back and put her arms around him. Fortunately, the sensible part was stronger.

* * *

'Welcome back,' Karen said when Regan walked in to the A&E department on her first day back. 'We've missed you. How's Georgie?'

'Doing really well, thanks,' Regan said. 'She's um . . . She's staying over with her father tonight.'

The department had been a buzz of chatter and clattering, but silence fell. Regan turned around. Josie was standing behind her with her mouth hanging open and Mike was behind the desk, the phone clasped in his hand.

'You're back together!' Josie squealed. 'Wheee! Congratulations, Regan. I just knew you two were meant to be together. This is wonderful news.'

Everyone was smiling now, practically queuing up to congratulate her. For a split second she felt a rush of warmth. If only it were true! But the truth was they had called an uneasy truce; and when they met, which was often, they barely had two words to say to each other. Bram had even taken on another vet so he'd have more time to spend with Georgie, and the new guy was living in his old camper van.

'No, no, we're not. We're really not,' Regan said quickly.

'Oh.' Josie looked really disappointed. 'Is there any chance?'

236

'None whatsoever.'

'I thought Georgie's father lived away,' Karen said.

'He's come back,' Regan said. 'You met him.'

'Bram,' Josie said, and now Karen looked astounded.

'The lifeboat guy?' she said. 'Him? He's Georgie's father? That stubborn idiot?'

Regan felt she should leap to his defence, but Karen had a point. 'I mean,' Karen went on, 'you had a relationship with that guy and you let him go?' She laughed incredulously. 'I mean he might be stubborn and everything, but he is gorgeous.'

'I know,' Josie said. 'Mad, isn't it.'

Suddenly Mike was striding across the floor, coming to the rescue. 'Haven't you got work to do?' he said briskly. 'Let's keep gossip out of the workplace, shall we? Welcome back, Regan.' Karen and Josie scattered in opposite directions and Mike pressed his hand between Regan's shoulders and steered her to one side. 'You all right? You're sure you're ready for this?'

'More than ready.'

'Good.' He looked over the top of her head and his expression darkened. 'No! Out you go. There's nothing wrong with you.'

Regan spun round and saw Stanley Bishop shuffling in. His mouth turned up in a smile when he saw her, but was quickly replaced with a grimace. 'Have a heart,' Regan said. 'He looks ill.'

'I know what's been going on here, Regan,' Mike said. 'When you were first off, he kept coming in looking for you. You're a soft touch and he knows it. He must have seen you coming to work and followed you. We can't accept waifs and strays, you know that. We're a busy emergency department.'

'I'll see to him,' she said.

'No,' Mike said, 'you won't. I'll get rid of him and you can see to the woman in cubicle five.'

But Stanley looked really ill. Worse than usual. The weather had been harsh and he was an old man. She could see Mike's point, but Stanley was a special case. She was very fond of him. They all were. Except Mike!

From a distance she watched as Stanley turned around and shuffled back out of the doors. Then she waited until Mike had gone into his office before running out behind him. The poor old guy was leaning against the wall outside.

'Stanley,' she called. He turned and coughed. 'Do me a favour and take some of this loose change off my hands,' she went on. 'It's weighing me down.'

'No, you're all right, love,' he said. He was so shaky. So unsteady on his feet. 'I don't want to get you in any trouble. Keep your money, pet. I've no appetite anyway.' He closed his cold, rough hands around hers and squeezed. When he coughed, it sounded as if he was bringing his lungs up. Regan put her arm around him and he felt so thin and frail through his clothes. There hadn't been anything of him to start with, but he'd lost weight.

'Come back inside,' she said. 'It's bitterly cold out here. Let's get you checked out.'

'No!'

'Yes,' she said. 'I insist.'

'What about your boss?'

'Let me worry about him.' She realised that she had the luxury now of going against the rules and to hell with the consequences. Bram would make sure Georgie didn't go without if she lost her job.

She took him back in and they made painfully slow progress to a cubicle. Once inside, she pulled the curtain around and helped him onto the bed. 'I'll get Karen to come and check you out,' she said, stooping to pull off his boots. His socks were soaking wet and as she peeled them off, she saw ulcers on his legs. 'How long have they been like this?'

'Don't know.'

She swished back the curtain and

walked right into Mike. 'What's he doing in here?'

'He's ill.'

'Get him out.'

'No!'

'Hey, Regan,' Josie called. 'Bram's here.'

'Bram?'

'He's got Georgie with him.'

Oh, great start. She'd already managed to annoy Mike, and now she was annoying him even more. Presumably Bram had been called out on an emergency and planned to dump Georgie here. Why hadn't he taken her to Lally's, as they'd agreed if anything came up?

'Go,' Mike said. 'Sort it out. I'll check the old malingerer over.'

Bram was waiting at reception, chatting to Karen. Regan pushed back a twinge of jealousy as the two of them laughed about something. It wasn't that she cared what Bram got up to — more that she felt so keenly what she was missing.

'Mummy!'

'Sorry about this,' Bram said. 'Georgie

left her toy cat in your car.'

'Did she? Oh no. She was so excited about staying over at your place, she must have forgotten. I should have remembered even if she didn't.'

'You had a lot on your mind,' he said. 'First shift back at work.'

'I'll get my keys.' She hurried off and when she came back, he was still chatting to Karen. They seemed to be getting along very well, considering she'd thought him stubborn and had put him firmly in his place when they met before.

'I'm parked — '

'I know,' he said, and his smile when he turned it from Karen was nothing short of dazzling. But the shine went off it as their eyes met and he realised who he was smiling at. This was their life now: icy politeness and no smiles. 'I saw it in the car park. I'll bring these right back. Georgie, stay here for a moment, honey.'

Karen leaned over and whispered in Regan's ear: 'It's official. You are insane!' Regan watched him walk away and couldn't help but agree. But it was too late now to do anything about it. A few minutes later, she watched him leave with Georgie skipping along beside him. She was holding his hand and didn't even look back. It was good that she was getting on so well with him, but at the same time Regan feared for the future. She'd killed whatever feelings he might have had for her stone dead, and now he was free to move on. Sooner or later he'd meet someone else, and she couldn't help but look in Karen's direction when she thought that. Karen was watching him too, a silly look on her normally very composed face. Perhaps he'd have more children and Georgie would become part of their family. It would be Regan left out in the cold and really, wasn't it what she deserved?

'Right, I've sent him for x-rays,' Mike said. 'And I've ordered tests, but it's pneumonia, Regan. No doubt in my mind. I'm going to try to get him a bed and — '

Regan was shaken from her thoughts. 'Is this Stanley we're talking about?'

'Seems the old duffer is really ill this time,' he said. 'You were right, Regan. I should have listened to you, but I know all about his overnight stays when I'm not around, so you can't blame me for being suspicious.' She gave him a sheepish grin. 'Did you really think I was unaware of what was happening in my own department?' he went on. 'That, by the way, does not give you carte blanche to open the doors to every homeless person that needs a bed for the night.' He softened his warning with a smile.

'What happens to him now?'

'Well he'll have a bed here for a few nights and I'll do all I can to get him a place in Rosemary House. If he'll stay there.'

'I'm sure he will. He's had enough, Mike. Poor old boy.'

'I'm sure he has.'

She made to walk away, but he caught her arm. 'Regan, wait.'

'Yes?' She smiled and stiffened. Mike

had that look in his eye again. He'd asked her out before a couple of times before Bram turned up, and she'd always said no.

'I was wondering if you were free this weekend. I'm going to — '

'I'm sorry, Mike,' she said.

'Yes, I know. Childcare and everything. But now Georgie's father is back on the scene and doing his bit, I thought perhaps you and I . . . '

She could see a happy, rosy future for Bram, but not for herself. She liked Mike, but knew it could never be more than that. To give him even the slightest hope would be downright cruel.

'No,' he said without her having to say a word. 'I understand. Probably best to keep it out of the workplace anyway.'

'Absolutely,' she said, relaxing. 'Sorry, Mike, really I am. I'm very fond of you, but — '

'Not in that way,' he finished for her.

She hugged him. In a different life, maybe, but she would never love any man as much as she loved Bram.

13

Bram had got back to his car only to find his keys weren't in his pocket, so he and Georgie had doubled back. 'There they are,' he said, spotting the keys on the ground outside the hospital. He bent to scoop them up and looked in the window. The lights were bright in there — shining down on Regan and Mike having a cosy hug.

Hah, it didn't take her long, did it? But maybe there was something there before he had come back. The closeness they'd shared that night, wonderful as it was, was a fluke. They were both emotional, tired and in need of comfort, that was all it was.

'It's snowing,' Georgie said, holding out her hand palm up and catching the flakes as they drifted down. 'Can we make a snowman?'

Bram laughed. 'If it settles, maybe

tomorrow,' he said. 'But we'll have to put a plastic bag over your cast to keep it dry.'

'It's itchy,' she said.

'I know, but it'll be off soon.'

Her little hand slid into his and they hurried across the car park. The snow began to fall harder and it was building up on the car windscreens and on the grass verge.

* * *

Regan kept an eye on the weather through the night and watched with increasing trepidation as the snow built up outside. At least she knew Georgie was safe with Bram. At the end of her shift she popped up to the ward to see Stanley, who was looking very comfortable and snug in bed.

'I think I came in the nick of time,' he said with a glance at the window. 'It hasn't stopped all night. Thank you for coming out to get me. I don't know what would have happened if I'd had to spend another night out, especially in this weather.'

Regan had a pretty good idea and it didn't bear thinking about. 'We're going to try to get you a place in a residential home. I know you're against it in principle, but — '

'Not any more,' he said. 'I've had enough, Regan. I'm too old to carry on like this.'

'I shan't argue with that,' she said. 'At least when you have a proper address I'll be able to come and visit you.'

'You'd do that?'

'Of course. And now I'd better set off home. Get plenty of rest and do everything they tell you.'

'Yes, boss,' he said.

It would be hard for him, she knew, adapting to life in a residential home, but he wouldn't survive the winter living rough.

'Drive carefully,' he said.

'Yes, boss,' she laughed.

She was shaking by the time she got to the doors. Few things really terrified her, but one thing that did was snow and ice. She hated driving in such bad conditions, and the drive down the hill to Coastguard Cottages was particularly treacherous. Their road was always the last one that got gritted, if it was done at all.

The snow was still coming down and it was still dark as she picked her way carefully across the car park. Her car was buried beneath a layer of white, but she could take her time clearing it off. Georgie was staying with Bram until the afternoon, and Bonnie was there too. No doubt his new vet would look after the surgery. Bram was really serious about being a good father.

Then she saw the headlight beams of a car parked nearby and realised someone was getting out. Bram! 'What's wrong?' she called. 'Is it Georgie?'

'She's fine. She's right here.'

She slithered towards him, almost falling over. 'What were you thinking, bringing her out in this weather?'

'Actually, I was thinking about how

you used to hate driving in the snow,' he said. 'And I thought you might appreciate a lift. My car sticks to the road like glue. I got it for all conditions, from snow to muddy fields.'

She could have hugged him. But . . . 'I need my car for work tonight.'

'If this keeps up, you won't be able to drive to work tonight,' he said. 'Not in that little thing. Jump in the back with Georgie; I'm taking you home.'

No point whatsoever arguing with that. She got into the back of the car. It was very warm inside and the windows were all clear. It would have taken ages to get the windows in her car to de-mist and for the heater to actually start working.

Georgie was well wrapped up. Bram had remembered her hat, scarf and gloves. 'Hello, Mummy! Will you help us make a snowman?'

Bram looked over his shoulder. 'Mummy has to rest,' he said. 'But we can build one for her while she's asleep.'

'You're going the wrong way,' Georgie said as instead of heading for Coast-guard Cottages, he turned the car towards the surgery.

'No I'm not,' he said. 'I'm taking you home. You can sleep in Georgie's bed.'

'But . . . '

'I'm not driving down the hill to Coastguard Cottages even in this vehicle,' he said. 'And there's no point anyway. If you stay at my place, it'll be easier to get you to work tonight.'

She was going to snap at him, 'I don't need your help!' After all, she'd managed perfectly well all this time without him. She'd driven in the snow and ice and true, she always ended up shaking like a leaf, but she knew she could do it. Was it tremendously weak of her to lean on him now? To batten down her indignation and admit that yes, she actually liked having his help? If only he'd smile at her instead of always looking at her with that sad, serious expression on his face.

It was amazing to watch Georgie in

the flat. She'd made herself completely at home. Some of her toys were scattered about the place. And Bonnie was just the same, curled up on the sofa with Rags once she'd finished greeting Regan.

'Make yourself at home,' Bram said. 'You know where everything is if you want anything to eat. And I don't want to see you for at least eight hours.'

Dismissed, just like that. He was tying a carrier bag over Georgie's cast. How things had changed since the night she'd spent here when he'd insisted on making her breakfast. If she fell asleep in his bath now, he was likely to pour cold water over her head to wake her up.

He put coats on all the dogs, then they left. The flat felt very quiet. Regan pottered about, had a shower and made herself a cup of tea, then went to Georgie's room. She'd told Regan that Sue had helped Bram make it nice. Sue worked for him downstairs. Georgie had spent time with her a few times when Bram had been called down to an emergency. Georgie thought she was wonderful. 'She's so pretty, Mummy,' she'd said.

Georgie's room was lovely. It had been painted palest pink and Bram — or Sue — had stuck fairies and princesses around the walls. Bram was the most masculine of men; imagining him carefully sticking delicate little fairies around the room was a bit far-fetched. It had to have been Sue.

The curtains and bedcovers were girlie and feminine, and he'd even got a fluffy princess rug. It fell just short of being completely over the top. There were bookshelves already stocked with books, and a little white wardrobe and chest of drawers. Various cuddly toys were lined up on the bed.

Regan picked one up and, holding it, went to look out of the window that overlooked the back garden. It had stopped snowing and the sun was making the snow glisten. The dogs were bounding about having a wonderful time while Bram and Georgie worked on their snowman.

She turned to look back at the room. It was like something out of a magazine — beautifully done, but with a woman's hand.

She got into the bed, pulled the covers tightly around herself, and fell asleep.

'Matching noses,' Bram laughed as he lifted Georgie up to look in the hall mirror when they came in. It was like having a miniature version of himself: two red noses, two pairs of bright blue eyes. Then he pulled off her hat and as her dark hair fell down over her shoulders, she transformed into a mini-Regan. He flinched. This was how it would always be. She was a constant reminder of her mother, and she must have been a constant reminder to Regan of him over the past few years. It was wonderful and painful all at the same time.

He helped her off with her coat, hung all their wet things up in the cloakroom, then popped into the surgery to make sure everything was running smoothly. Back upstairs, he gave each of the dogs a good rub-down with a towel before peeking in at Regan. Bonnie rushed in and launched herself onto the bed before he could stop her.

He picked up her clothes and closed the door quietly. The bedcovers would need changing, since Bonnie was still quite damp, but no matter; he'd bought extras. He couldn't have done it without Sue's help. He had no idea what sort of things little girls liked and she'd brought in a magazine to work. The picture of a child's bedroom inside was just how he imagined a little girl's room should look. Sue had gone shopping with him and helped him choose the right things. He'd put it together on his own, painstakingly sticking up stickers and arranging things on the shelves. He wanted it to be right for his little girl. He wanted it to be perfect. And he must have got it right, because Georgie loved it.

He made hot milky cocoa and he and Georgie sat on the sofa together to watch television. She was educating him in all the latest things to watch and he was trying to remember it all.

Everything he'd ever done in his life up until now paled into insignificance beside being a father. This was one thing he had to get absolutely right. You didn't get second chances when it came to being a parent. You either got it right, or you didn't.

* * *

Lally sat down, her cold hands cupped around a mug of tea. The cats were sprawled around the sitting room. They hadn't ventured out in the snow at all, although occasionally one of them would go and have a look outside to see if it had cleared up yet.

'I suppose I should be making a move,' Len said reluctantly. 'I want to get home before dark.'

'You could stay,' Lally said with a grin. 'I have a spare bed.'

He grinned back at her. 'Probably

best I don't, love,' he said with a wink. 'It'd get your neighbours gossiping.'

'I don't care about gossip,' Lally said with a mischievous laugh. She put her mug down and got to her feet to see Len out. And suddenly she was standing right in front of him, so close she could feel the warmth of his breath on her forehead. He reached out for her and she stepped into his embrace. She hadn't so much as looked at another man since her husband had died. She'd never wanted to. But Len had awakened something within her that she'd thought long gone.

He tilted her chin with his finger and was about to kiss her when her phone rang. 'Oh,' she laughed nervously as she stepped away. 'Saved by the bell.'

'Who wants to be saved?' Len quipped.

She answered the phone and frowned. 'Katie?' she said. 'Hello, love. What? No! No, don't do anything silly.' She looked at Len, panic-stricken. 'I know how you're feeling, I really do, but this isn't the answer.'

'What is it?' Len said, and Lally shook her head at him. 'I'm coming up,' she said. 'Right now. Promise you won't do anything until I get there. Please, Katie. Keep talking to me. Will you do that, love?' She covered the phone and looked at Len. 'She's on the cliff. She says she's going to throw herself off. I'm going to try and talk her down.'

'We should call the police.'

'How? My landline isn't working and you don't have your phone with you, do you? I thought not. I can't hang up on her, Len. We'll call for help when we get there and see what the situation is. I don't want people charging up there and scaring her.' She spoke into the phone again. 'Are you still there, Katie? Listen, love, I'm going to keep talking to you, okay?' She nodded at Len and he helped her into her coat. At least it wasn't snowing now, although the sky was full of clouds.

Len's chest felt sore as they trudged up the hill towards the cliffs. Lally was hanging onto his arm, talking to Katie all the time, trying to keep her calm. That poor girl. Her grief was so raw. So painful.

Lally's voice was soft and comforting, yet firm. She sounded like someone who knew what she was talking about — and she was stopping Katie from jumping. When they got to the cliff, he could see Katie standing at the edge, her coat billowing out behind her, caught by the breeze. She wasn't wearing gloves and the hand clutching the phone against her ear was red. She turned as they approached and slipped the phone into her pocket.

'Don't come any closer,' she said.

'Katie, love,' Lally said gently. 'Come away from the edge. Please.' She passed her phone back to Len. He was about to call for help when it bleeped at him and the screen went dark. Oh, hell. Dead battery.

'I can't, Lally,' Katie said, and she looked over her shoulder and seemed to stumble a little.

Len took a step forward and Lally

clutched his sleeve. 'I know you're hurting,' she said to Katie.

'I just want him back, Lally,' Katie said, and her sadness wrenched at Len's heart.

'I know you do,' Lally said. 'But it's not your time, sweetheart. Come away from the edge now, please.'

'I can't.'

'I don't think you really want to jump,' Lally said. 'That's why you called me.'

Almost without Len noticing, Lally was edging closer and closer to Katie. The girl looked ready to collapse. She was shivering. She hadn't dressed properly for the cold. She'd dressed like someone who didn't give a damn.

'What about David?' Lally said. 'Have you seen him since . . . I mean . . . ?'

Katie shook her head from side to side and stumbled again.

'Maybe we should call him, love,' Lally went on. 'He's still very fond of you, you know. I know he wanted to get back together before . . . '

Katie let out a shriek of anger. 'Yes he

did, and I said no. I couldn't forgive him. Okay, he said it was just one night — but he betrayed me, Lally. I didn't know that Jay had heard us talking. He must have been so upset when he heard me tell David there was no chance.'

Her foot slipped and she almost went over. Lally gasped. Len sprang forward again. He checked out her footprints in the snow. No one else had been up on the cliffs today. It looked as if Katie had been staggering about all over the place, pacing up and down. It was a miracle she hadn't already fallen over the edge. But she had started out further up and now she wasn't at the worst part. What was he thinking? There was no good place to fall over the edge!

'You still love him, don't you?' Lally said.

'Of course I do!' Katie cried. 'I never stopped.'

'Let me call him,' Lally said. 'Please.'

'No.'

'Take my hand, love,' Lally said, reaching out. Len held his breath, then let it out when Katie reached out.

What happened next was so fast, it hardly registered.

One minute Lally was holding Katie's hand, and the next Katie was sliding backwards and both women disappeared from view.

Len ran to the edge, screaming Lally's name, and he almost collapsed with relief when he heard her call out: 'I'm all right! Soft landing!'

'Is Katie okay?'

'Yes,' Lally called. 'But she's out cold. I don't think she hit her head — I think she fainted.' They must have gone all the way to the bottom!

'How about you? Are you hurt, Lally?'

'No. It's not very steep here. We landed on the sand. I'm a bit sore.' She broke off for a second. 'But I haven't broken anything.'

'I'll get help!' he yelled. 'Hold on! Don't move!'

'I'm not going anywhere!' Lally shouted back and she tried to laugh, but he heard her choke on a sob.

14

Regan picked up her uniform. It smelled clean and fresh, and it had been ironed. She could hear laughter coming from the living room. She'd woken with Bonnie nuzzling at her face, and it had taken her a few seconds to remember where she was and realise she wasn't in her own bed.

Bram had left a dressing gown hanging on the door for her too. She pulled it on and went into the living room.

'We've made some cakes, Mummy,' Georgie said. 'Would you like one?'

They'd made dozens of cupcakes with swirly lurid-coloured icing and sprinkles on the top.

'We made rather a lot,' Bram said sheepishly. 'They taste a lot better than they look. You could take some into work with you.'

'I'd like that,' she said. 'Is it okay if I

have a quick shower?'

'Have a long one if you like,' Bram said. 'Dinner won't be ready for another hour.'

'Dinner?'

'You didn't think I'd send you to work on an empty stomach, did you?'

'Bram's making toad-in-the-hole,' Georgie said. 'With roast potatoes and gravy.'

You could almost think they were a proper family, Regan thought as she showered. Almost. But Bram was pleasant to her only for Georgie's benefit. And he wasn't kidding about learning to cook properly.

The television was on in the living room when she came back dressed and ready for work, and the weather was the main topic on the news. It had caught everyone on the hop and most of the country was unprepared for the severity of it. 'I haven't seen snow like this here for years,' Regan said. 'It's very unusual. I don't want you driving me to work tonight, Bram. I'll walk in from here. It's not far.'

'You'll never make it on foot,' he said.

'I'm not sure you'll be able to drive either,' she replied. 'They said not to go out unless your journey is really necessary.'

'And it's necessary to get you to work, don't you think?' he said. 'You'll be needed at the hospital.'

She stared at him. He was wearing a thick cream Arran sweater and jeans, and his hair was slightly tousled. 'Something wrong?' he asked.

'No,' she said quickly. 'I was miles away.' Remembering how good it felt to be in his arms, and realising that it was never going to happen again — that was where she was.

'Sit with Georgie,' he said. 'Dinner won't be long.'

'Are you sure you'll be okay to have Georgie again tonight?' she said. 'I could get in touch with Lally . . .'

'Of course I'm sure. Doug will be here and if I do have to help out in the surgery, Sue will keep an eye on Georgie. They get on really well.'

'So I gather,' she said. Damn! She hadn't meant to sound so snippy. But she didn't want to think too much about Sue. Sue with the pretty face and long black eyelashes — that was how Georgie described her.

She could see through into the kitchen and watched Bram as he worked. How he'd changed from the guy that used to buy ready meals to put in the microwave. She'd changed too. Five years was a long time.

'Do you have to go to work, Mummy?'

'Yes, darling, but it won't be for much longer. I'm changing my shifts so I'll be home more and working when you're at school. You'll be able to go back to school once your cast is off. Are you looking forward to it?'

'Yes, I miss my friends. I miss . . . ' Her eyes filled with tears.

The doctor had advised keeping her at home until her arm was out of the cast. They wanted her to have time to come to the terms with Jay's death too.

The school had been very helpful, sending work home so that she wouldn't fall behind. It had helped so much, too, with Georgie's bonding with Bram. Not that they needed help in that department.

Regan put her arm around her and pulled her close. 'Hey,' she said, 'it's all right. Everything will be okay.'

Bram had just put their food on the table when his phone rang. Regan watched his face go pale. He looked at her, then away. 'I understand,' he said. 'Hold tight. I'm on my way.'

Regan was already rising to her feet. 'What's happened?'

He grabbed her arm and pulled her into the kitchen. 'It's Lally,' he whispered. 'There's been an accident. I have to go.'

'I'm coming too.'

'No, you stay here with Georgie.'

'But if Lally's hurt, I can be of more use than you,' she said. 'You stay here with Georgie.'

He looked at her for a split second,

then picked up the phone and spoke to Sue. It seemed like only seconds later that footsteps pounded up the stairs from the surgery, then a middle-aged woman burst in. She had big eyes and enormous long black eyelashes and she was pretty, but she was probably old enough to be Bram's mother.

'You sure about this, Sue?' Bram said.

'Of course I am!'

'Let's go,' he said, gathering up his gloves and hat.

'Go,' Sue said kindly when Regan hesitated. 'I'll look after Georgie. We've spent a bit of time together and she'll be fine with me. I'll stay here while she eats her dinner and then she can come downstairs. I'll bring her back up to the flat when we close and I'll stay with her until you get back.'

Georgie was perfectly happy with Sue, and Regan looked questioningly at Bram as she pulled on a pair of his tracksuit trousers that he'd insisted she wear. They drowned her, but at least she'd be warm.

'A couple of times when Georgie's been here, I've been called in to help out downstairs,' Bram said with an impatient huff. 'She's been fine with Sue.'

'I didn't say anything.'

'You didn't have to, Regan. Your face says it all.'

'As it happens, my face says nothing! Georgie's mentioned Sue to me several times. She's very fond of her.'

'So am I,' he said. 'She's been great. She even helped me choose the stuff for Georgie's room.'

'I guessed you hadn't done it on your own.'

'Thanks a bunch.' Bram pretended to look hurt and he came close to smiling, then he turned and ran down the stairs.

The snow was deeper than ever. Bram flung open the door of his four-by-four.

'You're not driving in this?' she said.

'Have you got a better idea?' he said. She hadn't. 'Then get in. We're wasting time.'

'What happened, do you know?' she said as they set off.

'It was Len who phoned,' Bram said. 'He was hardly making any sense. I don't know where he was calling from — he said something about not having his mobile with him and the landlines being down. Knowing Len, he was knocking on doors as soon as he came to houses and asking to use their mobiles.'

He drove out carefully. The car struggled a little at first, but he eased it over the snowy roads. Every time the wheels snatched or they slid a little, Regan gripped her seat, gritted her teeth and squeezed her eyes shut. 'So what did he say?' It was like getting blood out of a stone.

'It seems Lally and Katie went over the cliff.'

'What?'

'Now don't overreact,' he said calmly. 'It wasn't at the very high part, but further down where the fall isn't great . . . '

'You can't dress up something like

that, Bram! What the hell were they doing on the cliff in this weather?'

'Len said something about Katie intending to throw herself off.'

'Oh, no.'

'It's a long shot, but you haven't got Katie's husband's number, have you?'

'I do, as it happens,' she said. 'He called me after . . . after . . . ' She couldn't say it. 'I kept his number anyway. It's in my phone. Do you think I should ring him?'

'Yes. If it was . . . someone I cared about — and he clearly still cares about her — I'd want to know.'

The back end of the car slid and he righted it again with no fuss and carried on as if nothing had happened. Regan gripped her seat even tighter. *What if we're killed?* she thought. *Who will take care of Georgie?* They were going to the rescue of the one other person in the world she would trust to take care of her daughter.

'Don't worry,' Bram said as if he'd read her mind. 'We're all going to get through this. I wouldn't have let you come along if I thought it was danger-ous.'

'You don't own me, Bram.'

'I didn't say I did, but Georgie needs a mother and I'll do everything in my power to protect hers. Make that call, Regan.'

David answered. She didn't know him all that well, but he always seemed nice. She knew he'd had a fling with a woman from work and that Katie hadn't been able to forgive him. She knew too that he'd wanted to come back, but Katie wouldn't have him. Quickly she told him what had happened. 'Can you get down here?'

'I'll leave right away. I'll get there somehow. How bad is she hurt?'

'I don't know yet, David,' she said. 'Just drive carefully.'

Bram had turned onto the road that led up to the cliffs. In the distance Regan could see the figure of a man waving his arms. 'There's Len!'

There was no wind, but clouds

obscured the moon. If the wind picked up and it started to snow again, it would soon turn into a blizzard. The last place you wanted to be in a blizzard was at the top of a cliff. But it wasn't windy and it wasn't snowing — yet. Regan's stomach knotted.

Len ran towards them and fell flat on his face in the snow. Bram stopped the car and jumped out. Regan followed. By the time they reached him, Len was struggling to his feet.

'Thank God,' he said. 'This way, quick! It was Katie,' he went on breathlessly. 'She called Lally and said she was going to jump. She thinks she's got nothing to live for.' He broke off and clutched at Bram's arm. 'You've got to help them, Bram. They've fallen all the way to the bottom.'

'Is help on the way?'

'You're it,' Len said. 'The emergency services are stretched to the limit and they're going to get here as soon as they can, but right now, we're their only hope.'

'It should be sandy at the bottom at this point,' Regan said, trying desperately to get her bearings, trying to remember what the tides were doing.

'Lally said they'd landed on the sand. She thought Katie had fainted, but hadn't hit her head.'

'Good.'

'I'll bring the car up closer,' Bram said. 'I've got ropes in the back.'

Regan stared at him in shock. Her best friend was down there and now the father of her child planned to go over the edge.

'The tide will be in too far to go round via the beach. This is the only way,' Bram said. That was right. Regan visualised the beach. The cliffs dipped in here and people often got caught on the little patch of beach, trapped by the incoming tide.

'Regan?'

'Do what you have to do, Bram.'

This wasn't the section of cliff where Jay and Georgie had gone over. It wasn't as steep, and the rocks not as sheer. And if Lally and Katie had fallen without injuring themselves, then Bram going over with a rope would be much safer. He wound the rope around his middle.

'We should wait for the helicopter,' Len said.

'You called me up here,' Bram said, 'because you know as well as I do that we can't afford to wait.' He fastened the rope to the tow bar, then Len moved the car until the rope was taught. 'Take it slow, Len!' Bram yelled. 'Regan, you're going to have to guide him.'

There wasn't time to think. Regan nodded and lifted her hand, ready to give Len the signal to reverse. The car jerked back and Bram went over the side. She heard him swear, then shout, 'Tell him to slow down!' But she was already running to the car.

'I'll do it,' she said. 'Your feet are cold and you're shaken up. Get out, Len. You guide me.'

'My foot slipped on the clutch,' Len said as he climbed out. 'I can hardly feel my feet. Is he okay?'

'Yes. Go back and call directions.' She got behind the wheel. It was a big car and although driving on the snow and ice scared the life out of her, she knew that this thing had great traction, so long as you kept it steady. No harsh movements.

It was agonising inching back so slowly, until at last Len put up his hand. 'Stop!' She pulled on the brake and jumped out and went as close to the edge as she dared. It was impossible to see the people below, but Regan could see the waves getting closer and closer to the shore. It wouldn't be long before it was full tide. Once it reached them, they wouldn't have a hope in hell of surviving.

'I'm sending Katie up first!' Bram yelled. 'She's conscious and scared. I don't think anything's broken.'

'Watch her back and neck, Bram,' Regan called out.

It seemed an age before Bram called up that they were ready. 'Slow as you

can!' he shouted. 'No sudden movements.'

'You do it,' Len said. 'I'll guide you.
You're a smoother driver than I am.'

Regan took a few deep breaths, then
began to drive slowly away from the
cliff edge. Her knees were shaking with
fear, but she managed to keep the
clutch steady as the big car rolled
forward, snow crunching beneath the
tyres. She tried not to think about Katie
dangling on the end of the rope, and
when Len yelled 'Stop!' she let out her
breath in a long hiss, then ran back
to the edge as Len was helping Katie
over the edge. She was sobbing, but
mercifully uninjured.

'I'm sorry,' she wept. 'I'm so sorry. I
slipped. I didn't mean to . . .'

Regan wrapped blankets around her
and held her close. 'Don't be sorry.
You've been through hell. And listen,
David's coming. He's going to get here
as soon as he can.'

'I still love him, Regan,' Katie wept.
The bitter, scratchy, bad-tempered

woman she'd become had gone, and all that remained was a frightened shell. 'If I'd only got over my hurt and taken him back . . . '

'Don't think like that, Katie. You can't change the past, but you can do something about the future. You and David . . . you need each other now.'

Soon it was time to do it again, this time bringing Lally up to the top. *This doesn't get any easier*, Regan thought as she moved the car again.

When they pulled Lally onto the top, she gasped, 'Hurry! The water's almost in. It's coming in so fast.'

Len threw the rope over the side and Regan ran back to the car. It would be quicker this time. Bram fastening himself to the rope wouldn't take as long as it had with Katie and Lally. Len gave her the signal and Regan began to creep forward, resisting the urge to put her foot down and get him up as soon as possible.

She'd hardly moved a few metres when the car jerked forward and Len let out a shout. Katie was beside the car, hammering on the window. 'The rope broke!' she screamed.

'What?'

'Len saw it had frayed, but it was too late.'

There wasn't enough rope to send down more — and worse than that: when Regan shouted out, Bram didn't answer. 'No!' she cried. 'No, you are not doing this to us, Bram Fletcher.' She thrust the car keys at Len. 'Get down to the town,' she instructed as she fished a first-aid kid out of the car and stuffed it in a backpack she found in the boot. 'Alert the lifeboat crew. Take Lally and Katie with you and get them to hospital as soon as you can.'

'What are you going to do? You're not planning to climb down there?' he said.

'Are you kidding?' she said. 'I'm scared of heights. There's no way I could go down. No, I'm going down to the end, then I'll make my way back across the rocks.'

'Are you out of your mind?'

'You grew up around here, Len. You must have played on the cliffs as a child, and you know it's possible to go along the face of the cliffs. You must have done it when you were a kid. For a dare?'

He looked at her as if she was mad. 'No,' he said. 'I never did. I was never that stupid!'

'Have you got any better ideas?'

'We can't let you do it,' Lally said.

'I have to! If he gets taken by the tide, he doesn't stand a chance. If I can get to him before the sea does, I can help him get higher up the cliff and we'll wait for rescue.'

Lally looked at Len.

'He's not answering us, love,' Len said to Regan, his voice calmer. 'How are you going to get an unconscious man up the cliff?'

'I'll think of something,' she said, tightening the straps of the backpack. 'Please, hurry.'

Running down the hill through the snow was hard going. The muscles in her legs protested and with every gasp of cold air, her chest hurt. But thinking of Bram lying at the foot of the cliffs kept her going. Nothing else mattered but getting to him.

She was doing this for Georgie. She wasn't going to let her little girl lose her father all over again.

At the bottom of the slope, she jumped down onto the beach and doubled back, scrambling over the rocks until she could get no further. She felt no pain as she smashed down again and again. Her body already hurt with the cold. Not once did she think she might not make it herself. It didn't even cross her mind that she wouldn't get back to Georgie. In the car it had been different; she hadn't been in control. Now she was. She was running on adrenaline.

She had to go upwards. Up and along. She climbed up above the water and began to move sideways. Progress was painfully slow, but if she went faster she risked slipping, and she had absolutely no intention of killing herself.

At last the cliff bowed inwards, sheltering the last remaining patch of sand. She looked up. It wasn't that high. If they helped each other, she could get Bram up there. No problem! Easy peasy! She choked back a burst of desperate laughter. The clouds parted as she jumped down onto the sand and the moon ignited the sky, gleaming down on the waves as they washed over the shore, but she couldn't see Bram; couldn't tell which one of the dark shadows at the base of the cliff might be him.

Then one of the shadows spoke. 'Regan? What the hell are you doing down here?'

'Coming to get you,' she said. 'Len's alerting the lifeboat in case we can't make it back up.'

Of all the places to fall, this was probably the best. If they couldn't get up the cliff, the lifeboat would be able to get pretty close to them here. Or they could go back the way she'd come, scrambling across the cliff face like a pair of crabs. She almost laughed again. The situation wasn't nearly as bad as she'd feared.

She knelt on the sand beside him, water lapping at her heels, and felt the stickiness of blood on his head. *But that's okay*, she told herself. *Heads bleed a lot, that's what they do;* she knew that.

'I don't know what happened,' he said. 'One minute I was coming back up the cliff, the next I woke up with my mouth full of sand.'

'Well, you're okay now,' she said. 'We're going to climb up. If you can't make it all the way, we'll go as far as we can and wait for rescue.'

'You go ahead,' he said. 'I'll wait down here.'

'What?' She laughed. 'Don't be mad! This'll be underwater in a few minutes.'

'Yeah, well, I can admire the view better from down here. Oh darn, I forgot — you borrowed some of my trousers. I hope you haven't torn them.'

'What are you talking about?' she said, baffled. 'Come on, Bram. You're not making any sense. On your feet.' She grabbed his arm and tried to pull, but he wasn't budging. 'What is wrong with you?' she yelled. 'Why are you playing the fool? Get up, will you?'

'I can't.' His voice cracked. 'Get back up the top. Leave me here. Do it, Regan.'

'What? Why? Stop being such an idiot.' He gripped her wrist tight. She tried to pull away but couldn't. 'You're hurting me, Bram.'

'Go,' he said, releasing her. 'Georgie needs you.'

She caught her breath and looked up. The waves were getting bigger as they smashed over the rocks, showering them with icy cold spray. 'I'll follow you,' he said. 'I just need to get my breath back.'

She almost believed him. Almost. But there was no way the Bram Fletcher she knew would have sent her on her own up the cliff. He'd have wanted to be there, ready to catch her. It didn't matter what his personal feelings were; to men like Bram they were of no consequence. His drive was to save life at all costs.

She ran her hands down his leg. 'Hey,' he said. 'This is no time for that sort of thing.'

'Shut up, Bram.'

As she ran her hands down his other leg, he reached out again, clamping his hand over her wrist, but she wrenched her hand free and felt his ankle, trapped between two rocks.

15

'Oh my God,' she whispered.

'Now will you go?' he said softly.

'No!' She clawed at the sand around the rock, then tried to shift it. It could go down forever beneath the sand.

'You're not getting me out of here without the use of a JCB,' he said. 'So do the sensible thing and go while you can.'

'I'm not leaving you,' she said.

'Now who's being a reckless idiot? Do as you're told for once in your life, woman.'

'Would you leave someone trapped down here?'

His silence was all the answer she needed. She clawed again at the sand around the rock. As soon as she dug into it, the hole filled with water, a sure sign that they would soon be overwhelmed. She wrapped her arms round the rock and tried to pry it loose, but it didn't budge.

'Please,' he said. 'I'll be fine. The sea might loosen the rocks, then I'll be able to get out.'

She grabbed his leg and pulled and he groaned in agony. It must be broken. Brute force wasn't going to do it, and making him pass out with pain certainly wasn't going to help.

'See sense will you?' he grated. 'Go now, while you still can.'

'We'll wait for the lifeboat,' she said.

'They can't get the damn boat in this close until the tide's higher. By then it'll be too late for either of us.'

'You think you're the only man alive with enough determination to save lives?' she said. 'If you were doing this rescue, you'd find a way, wouldn't you?' She amazed herself at how calm she sounded when inside she was anything but. She was scared out of her wits — mainly for him, a little for herself, and a lot for Georgie. But while she was alive and breathing, she just couldn't contemplate not making it.

'Regan,' he said. 'About us . . . '

'There is no us, remember?'

'But there should have been. We used to be happy before I had that damn accident. It wasn't just because of your ultimatum that I left. They told me I might never walk again. I wanted to leave, to get out of your life before you felt duty-bound to stay with me.'

'What?' If he hadn't been so hurt and helpless, she would have hit him! 'How dare you say that?' she cried. 'Do you really think I was so shallow that I'd stop loving you because you were in a wheelchair? What sort of person do you take me for?'

'I know you would have stuck with me,' he said. 'And that was the problem. You made it easy for me to walk . . . wheel myself away and blame you.'

'I loved you, you idiot,' she sobbed. 'After you'd gone . . . ' Oh what was the point? It was all too late now.

'I've never stopped loving you, Regan,' he murmured. 'You should know that. I'm sorry I've been so angry with you.' His voice slurred.

'Hey,' she pushed him. 'Don't go to sleep. If I'm staying here with you, you are damn well not going to die on me, do you hear?' His head rested against her shoulder and she pushed him upright. 'Stay with me, Bram!' she shouted. 'Stay with me.'

'Why?'

'Because I love you, you stupid great lump! I love you and I don't want to lose you.'

'Knew it,' he laughed weakly.

'So why didn't you come back?' she asked, licking her lips. She had to keep him talking; keep him conscious. 'You know, when you found out you were going to be okay? Why not just come back?'

'It took nearly two years, Regan, and I wasn't a nice person to know while I was recovering.'

'I can imagine,' she said. 'You were never the best patient.'

'I'd kept in touch with Dennis and a

couple of times he said he wanted to tell me something about you. I told him I didn't want to hear it. I thought . . . ' He broke off and she heard him swallow. 'I thought he meant you'd found someone else. I told him I wasn't interested and what you did was of no consequence.'

She brushed his hair away from his face, gently moving it out of the blood so she could put on a dressing. 'I should have tried to find you,' she said. He dropped his head to her shoulder again and she pushed him upright. 'Do. Not. Sleep!' she yelled. 'Bram!'

'There,' Len said as he turned the beam on the beach and saw a figure jumping up and down waving their arms. Regan. 'We'll take the *Molly Jane* in as far as we can.'

Four of the men climbed out of the boat and waded through the thigh-deep water to the beach. There was no beach left. Bram was sitting in the water. Regan was crouching beside him.

'His foot is trapped,' she said. 'And

his ankle is broken.'

'This is going to hurt you more than it's going to hurt me,' Malcolm said with a laugh.

'I bet you say that to everyone,' Bram laughed back.

It took them less than five minutes to free his foot and when they did, Bram bellowed with pain and Malcolm, despite his earlier words, apologised with a crack in his voice.

Watching from the boat, Len saw two of the guys lift Bram up and start their unsteady journey back to the boat. Behind him came the other two, carrying Regan.

'What were you thinking, Len?' Bram said the minute he was aboard. 'Letting her do that? She could have been killed.'

'Thanks for coming to my rescue, Len,' Len said. 'Oh, that's okay, Bram me old mate. Any time.'

Bram glared at him for a moment, then roared with laughter. Len clapped him on the shoulder. 'Good to have you back, son,' he said.

'Someone here to see you,' Lally said as she stepped through the curtain. Katie turned her face into her pillow. 'I don't want to see anyone,' she mumbled.

'I hope you'll see me,' David said as he stepped up to the bed. He smiled at Lally and she nodded and withdrew.

'What are you doing here?'

'Regan called me,' he said.

'You didn't have to come.'

'But I did. When I asked you if we could try again, I — '

'We had Jay then,' she said. 'It was different. There's nothing left.'

'What about love? I still love you, Katie. I think . . . I think we should be together, now more than ever.'

'You're just saying that,' she murmured, voice leaden with misery. 'You feel sorry for me.'

'No,' he said. 'I feel sorry for myself. For what I've lost; for what I threw away. This was my fault, all of it.'

'It wasn't. It was mine. I should have

let you come back when you asked, but I wanted to make you suffer . . . Well I certainly did that.' She broke into sobs and David sat on the bed and hugged her.

'We can go on blaming ourselves for the rest of our lives, or we can start over. Will you come back with me when I leave, Katie? I'll take care of you, I swear, and I will never hurt you again.'

Lally stood on the other side of the curtain, her fingers crossed. She knew it was wrong to eavesdrop, but she wanted to be there in case Katie sent him away, so she could send him straight back in. She didn't hear what Katie said, but it was followed by a cascade of weeping and when she peeked in, they were holding each other as if they'd never let go.

Brushing away a tear, she hurried away from the ward. By the time she got to the corridor, she was sobbing herself. 'You're not that dismayed to see me, are you, Lally?' Len said, and she couldn't hold back. She ran into his arms. He smelled of salt and boats. 'We got them,' he told her. 'Bram's down in A&E now. They're both fine, apart from his smashed ankle that is.'

'And so are you,' she said. 'I'm so relieved.'

'Me?' he laughed. 'I'm always all right, me. I'm not the one throwing himself off cliffs.'

'Bram didn't exactly . . . '

'I'm talking about you, you brave, wonderful lady,' he said. And then he kissed her and Lally's world turned upside down, then righted itself again. She had never expected to fall in love again, but it seemed she had and it was wonderful.

★　★　★

After the snow came a brief relatively warm spell and a couple of days of rain. It soon washed the snow away and it only persisted in dirty little heaps where it had been piled up.

Regan held tight to Georgie's hand

and hurried along the hospital corridor. She hadn't been to visit Bram, although she'd been to the hospital to take Georgie to have her cast removed and a couple of times to visit Stanley, who was well on the road to recovery now. But she couldn't put off the inevitable any longer. Georgie was chomping at the bit wanting to see him. She'd insisted on buying him a balloon from the hospital shop. It said 'Get well, Daddy!' on it in big blue letters.

Regan stopped dead outside the ward. Now was not the time to have a panic attack. She hadn't been to see him since the night they were rescued. They'd said some daft things to each other in the heat of the moment and she was terrified he'd be regretting the things he said. And what if he'd been delirious with pain and didn't know what he was saying? It was foolish and premature to think she'd been forgiven.

'Come on, Mummy.' Georgie pulled on her hand and she winced a little. Her hands were bruised, her fingernails brutally short where they'd been smashed. She'd been completely shocked when she saw the extent of her injuries — all minor, thankfully, but hardly any part of her body had escaped unscathed. Bram had always said you didn't feel pain when you were on a rescue. At last she understood what he meant.

She took a deep breath and stepped into the ward.

He was sitting on the edge of the bed, reaching for his crutches, and one of the younger nurses was rushing over to him. 'Wait! What are you doing?'

'I'm going to the bathroom,' he said wearily.

'Let me help you. You're not supposed to . . . '

'I can manage perfectly well,' he said, pushing her well-meaning hands away. 'I don't need any help, thank you, love. I know you mean well, but I don't want anyone to hold my hand.'

The nurse's expression darkened. 'I have a job to do, and that includes making sure you don't fall over or collapse on your way to the bathroom.'

Georgie looked up at Regan and grinned.

'It's about time you learned to do as you were told, Bram Fletcher,' Regan said as they hurried over to the bed. His face lit up when he saw them. Well, Georgie anyway.

'A balloon,' he said. 'Brilliant!'

Regan stepped forward. 'I can leave you two for a while,' she offered. 'Make myself scarce. I'll come back for Georgie later. But Bram, if you need to go to the bathroom, accept the help on offer.' She turned, ready to make her escape, when his voice stopped her in her tracks.

'Get yourself back here,' he said. She turned slowly.

'I beg your pardon?'

'You heard,' he said. And then he grinned, and the ice in her heart melted as he patted the bed. 'Come and sit with us. We have a lot to talk about.'

'We do? I thought you needed the bathroom?'

'That was just a ploy.' He winked at the nurse. 'Sorry. I just wanted to get off the ward for a few minutes.'

'It's all right,' Regan told her. 'I'll make sure he behaves.' She moved closer and pulled up a plastic chair, sitting a safe distance away. Georgie sat on the bed, staring at the cast on Bram's foot.

'Want a pen?' he said, and she giggled. 'Yes, please.'

He'd already had a few people write on it and had a thick marker pen at the ready. Georgie carefully wrote her name, then enclosed it in a big wonky heart. 'That is fantastic,' Bram said. 'Now I need a hug! Have you got one for me?' She scrambled up and sat on his lap. She looked so cosy. Regan couldn't remember sitting on her dad's lap. Ever. 'I'm moving back into my old camper van,' he said, and Regan's heart jolted with alarm. Was he planning to move on again?

'Why?'

'I've agreed to let Doug move into the flat. He's been living in the van and going home at weekends, but he's keen to make his position permanent, and if he moves into the flat he'll be able to bring his wife and kids here.'

'But you can't stay in a camper van with a broken ankle.'

'Well, I can't leave it behind,' he said, and she couldn't help laughing along with him. 'I managed fine in the van before.'

'You are not sleeping in a camper van in this weather,' Regan said.

'Am I not?' His eyes shone with amusement.

'You can stay with us,' she said before she could stop herself.

'What about my dogs?'

'They can come too.'

'And cats?'

'Of course.'

'You are a very special lady, do you know that? It'll be a bit cramped, but it'll do until we get ourselves somewhere bigger.'

'What?'

'I'm sorry, Regan,' he said. 'Are your

ears still full of salt water?' He nudged Georgie when he said that and they both laughed.

'Let me get this straight. You think we should move in together?'

'You were the one who suggested it.' He looked at Georgie and did an exaggerated innocent shrug which made Georgie giggle even harder.

'No, I didn't . . . Well yes, I did, but who said anything about getting somewhere bigger?'

'I did.' He rolled his eyes. 'Keep up!'

Regan shook her head. Two pairs of identical blue eyes laughed merrily at her. 'We will of course have to get married.' When he said that, he did the biggest wink at Georgie and they both burst out laughing.

'This isn't funny,' Regan said. She was on her feet now, closer to the bed, her heart going wild behind her ribs. 'Stop it! Both of you! This is our future you're laughing and joking about. You can't turn everything into a game. Moving in together, getting married, it's all serious and . . . '

'Oh, for goodness sake, Regan,' he said and grabbed her, pulling her close and kissing her. She tried to wriggle free, to protest, but his lips were very insistent and somewhere in the background she could hear Georgie laughing and clapping. And it was a very nice kiss.

When he let her go, her eyes were still closed, her lips still parted. She ran her tongue over them, tasting him, wondering when she was going to wake up.

'When we were on the beach you said, and I quote, 'I love you, you stupid great lump! I love you and I don't want to lose you.' Were you just saying that, or did you mean it?'

She opened her eyes, still feeling wonderfully dizzy from his kiss. 'Of course I meant it,' she said.

He grabbed her hand and pulled her closer again. 'They're discharging me tomorrow. I've nowhere else to go. Well, apart from the cold, lonely camper van.'

Georgie tugged at Regan's sleeve. 'Say yes, Mummy!' Then she turned to

Bram. 'Can I call you Daddy now?'

Regan saw the laughter die in his eyes to be replaced with pain, sweet pain. 'Oh, honey,' he murmured. 'I would love it if you did. And you,' he said, squeezing Regan's fingers. 'I love you so much. I don't want to lose you again. Seriously. Will you marry me?'

Regan hugged him, resting her head against his chest, feeling the fast thud of his heart. Her big, brave man was afraid she'd turn him down. He kissed her head and murmured, 'I'll give up being a lifeboat man if that's what it takes.'

She gasped. 'You don't have to,' she said, tears trickling from her eyes. 'It won't make any difference.'

'Oh.' He sounded deflated and dejected. 'I see.'

'No, you don't see.' She straightened up and cupped his dear, battered face in her hands. 'I love you, Bram. Yes, I'll marry you — unconditionally.'

Georgie leapt off the bed and began to twirl around. 'I'm doing a happy dance!' she yelled. 'My mummy and

Daddy are getting married!'

A cheer went around the ward and patients and staff broke into spontaneous applause, but Regan could barely hear it for the singing in her heart.

They'd wasted far too much time already. The future was theirs, and from now on there'd be no looking back.

We do hope that you have enjoyed reading this large print book.

Did you know that all of our titles are available for purchase?

We publish a wide range of high quality large print books including:
Romances, Mysteries, Classics
General Fiction
Non Fiction and Westerns

Special interest titles available in large print are:
The Little Oxford Dictionary
Music Book, Song Book
Hymn Book, Service Book

Also available from us courtesy of Oxford University Press:
Young Readers' Dictionary
(large print edition)
Young Readers' Thesaurus
(large print edition)

For further information or a free brochure, please contact us at:
Ulverscroft Large Print Books Ltd.,
The Green, Bradgate Road, Anstey,
Leicester, LE7 7FU, England.
Tel: (00 44) **0116 236 4325**
Fax: (00 44) **0116 234 0205**

VALENTINE MASQUERADE

Margaret Sutherland

New Year's Eve is hot and sultry in more ways than one when a tall, handsome prince fixes the newest lady in his court with a magnetic gaze. Who could say no to a prince — especially a charmer like Will Bradshaw? Caitlin has to wonder. And Will wonders, too, if he might have finally found the woman to banish the hurts of years gone by. But what if the one ill-judged mistake of Caitlin's past happens to be the single fault he can't accept?

THE HOUSE ON THE HILL

Miranda Barnes

When a young man moves into the old house next door, Kate Jackson's curiosity is piqued. However, handsome Elek Costas is suspiciously reclusive, and the two get off to a bad start when he accuses her of trespassing. Whilst Kate is dubious of Elek's claim to be the rightful owner, her boyfriend Robert has his eye on acquiring the property for himself . . . Just what is the mystery of Hillside House? Kate is determined to find out!